ALSO BY
DARCY COATES

The
HAUNTING
of
ROOKWARD
HOUSE

DARCY COATES

Poisoned Pen
PRESS

Published by Poisoned Pen Press, an imprint of Sourcebooks
P.O. Box 4410, Naperville, Illinois 60567-4410
(630) 961-3900
sourcebooks.com

Originally self-published in 2017 by Black Owl Books.

Library of Congress Cataloging-in-Publication Data

Names: Coates, Darcy, author.
Title: Haunting of Rookward House / Darcy Coates.
Description: Naperville, Illinois : Poisoned Pen Press, [2020] | "Originally self-published in 2017 by Black Owl Books"--Title page verso.
Identifiers: LCCN 2019050862 | (trade paperback)
Subjects: GSAFD: Ghost stories.
Classification: LCC PR9619.4.C628 H43 2020 | DDC 823/.92--dc23
LC record available at https://lccn.loc.gov/2019050862

Printed and bound in the United States of America.
VP 10 9 8

CHAPTER 1

April 1965

AN AGED FLOORBOARD GROANED somewhere deep in the house. Thomas lay still in the bed but let his eyelids drift open. He knew he shouldn't give in to the paranoia, but it was hard at night when the branches scrabbled at the shingles like brittle fingernails and the wind rattled the doors as though demanding to be let inside.

A distorted shadow slid across the bedroom ceiling. Thomas tracked it without moving a millimeter, his slow breaths and racing heart in disharmony. Sweat made his palms itch.

Louise shifted at his side. Strands of her sandy-brown hair slid across her cheek as she made a low humming noise of disquiet at the back of her throat. Thomas wondered if she sensed it, too— the pall of unease that descended over the house nearly every night. The one that made him check on the children a dozen times in an hour, even though the baby monitor played only even, sleeping breaths into the room.

It's Amy. She's here again.

His itching palms became unbearable, and Thomas broke the stillness to squeeze his hands into fists. The floorboard groaned again, and he tried to tell himself it was only the wind tugging at the house, but it wasn't easy to disregard the muted warnings. Louise's brows were pulled together, and a muscle twitched in her jaw.

Thomas extended his feet over the edge of the bed. Only scattered patches of moonlight struggled through the clouds, leaving his room doused almost entirely in black. As his toes hunted across the wooden boards, a part of him expected to feel clammy, scabbed fingers fasten around them, with nails as long as the scratching tree branches and a grip like iron to drag him underneath the bed.

Instead, he found the soft wool of his footwear. He slid his feet inside with a silent exhale. The slippers were cool but would warm quickly. Thomas stood and wrapped his arms around his torso. His bathrobe hung nestled in the closet to his left, but he preferred to brave the cool air for a few moments rather than face the patch of death-black inside.

Monsters lurking under the bed. Evil living in his closet. They were childish fears, ones he'd thought he was long past before meeting Amy. But somehow, she'd brought them all back. Now, when his children begged him to check under their beds before they went to sleep, he had to steel himself for the task.

The baby monitor rested on the table closest to his side of the bed. He nudged the volume up a fraction and listened to three pairs of lungs working through the night. A few months before, when their youngest turned one, Louise had suggested they box it up and store it in the attic. But Thomas had insisted on keeping it in their room and changing its batteries regularly. He felt safer having that small measure of contact with his children, even when he couldn't see them. And Louise's complaints had fallen silent soon after she'd first seen Amy.

Thomas moved toward the window. He rolled his feet to keep from disturbing Louise, even though she was a deep sleeper. Tiny tendrils of frost coiled across the corners of the glass, and when he exhaled, Thomas's breath arced out in a cloud. He squinted into their yard, hunting among the patches of garden and the heavy shadows for signs of movement.

He could have sworn Louise had put a little violet plant in the corner of their stone-edged garden that morning. He'd seen her digging the hole, her floppy sun hat not quite large enough to hide her smile as she knelt in her sanctuary. And yet, the space he'd seen her working was now only bare dirt.

Maybe she found a better spot for it.

Thomas brought his thumb up to his mouth and worried at it. He never needed to clip his fingernails anymore; the compulsive habit kept them too short.

He moved his attention from the garden and toward the edge

of the woods. There were no clear patches of light and dark in there; the two shades tangled together into a riotous, hysterical mess where the speckles and flecks blended as the wind moved branches. It was madness to search for motion inside them, though he'd spent enough hours trying to.

A muffled, hiccupping gasp interrupted the smooth exhales floating through the baby monitor. Thomas picked up the blue instrument and rotated the volume switch to its highest setting. He stared at its speakers, waiting, holding his own breath. After a quiet moment, a woman spoke, so softly and smoothly that it sounded like an exhale: "Hush, baby."

Thomas's heart turned to lead. He dropped the monitor, and Louise's frown contracted as the one-way radio hit the floor with a resounding *thunk*. She didn't wake. Thomas tried to call to her, but his mouth was dust dry. He felt his heart restart, but with an aching pulse, the kind that hit his ribs and made bile rise in the back of his throat.

He dragged his feet into motion, instructing them to carry him past the closet and its inky black center, past the bed with its invisible scrabbling hands. He nudged Louise's shoulder but didn't wait for her to stir. His bedroom door creaked as he opened it. He hit his palm on the switch beside the door, and the hallway was filled with a light that should have felt comforting but somehow failed. The glow that came from the single bulb hung above his head couldn't reach far. Both the end of the corridor to his left and the twisting staircase to his right were left in shadows. It created a tiny oasis, though, and gave him the courage to quicken his pace toward the room beside his own.

The door was ajar. He'd shut it when he'd put the children to sleep—he was certain of it. Trembling fingers nudged at the wood, opening it further. Inside was nearly perfectly dark; he'd blinded himself with his oasis of hallway light, and the bulb's influence couldn't extend into his children's bedroom. He felt the wall beside the door, hunting for the switch he'd pressed a hundred times but could never seem to find at night.

"Thomas?" A floorboard groaned behind him as Louise, her voice clouded by sleep, approached. "You okay?"

He found the switch. Light doused the two beds and the crib, the toy chest, the wooden trains, the drawings taped to the walls, and the shelf of brightly colored books. Thomas realized he'd been holding his breath and drew one in a rush.

"Thomas?" Louise stopped just behind him. She didn't touch his shoulder, like she used to, but her presence was still a comfort. "What is it?"

"Heard something in the baby monitor." He stepped into the room. Dan, their oldest, wriggled onto his other side but didn't raise a fuss. Becca was still. And Georgie, nestled in the crib, continued to sleep.

He braced himself and bent to look under the beds. The spaces were empty, of course, like they always were.

Thomas stared at the baby monitor positioned on the edge of the crib then crossed to the closet. He tugged open the door and glanced across the paint-splattered clothes, the blankets, and the miniature suits and dresses reserved for Sundays. No monster lurked among them.

"Thomas. You're going to upset their sleep again." Louise leaned against the doorframe, her hair hanging about her face in disheveled loops. As she rubbed at the side of her nose, shadows highlighted the crease between her eyebrows.

"It wasn't a dream this time." Thomas closed the closet. He scanned the room, but there was nowhere else to look; there was barely enough room to walk since he'd moved all three beds into it. "I—I *thought…*"

Louise squeezed her mouth into a grim smile. Dark hollows around her eyes spoke to her own disturbed rest, and Thomas made a resigned noise.

"I'm sorry. I've been jumpy—"

"Thomas."

"And I know it's not fair to you or the kids—"

"Thomas." She reached toward him and waited until he took her hand before speaking again. "You can apologize tomorrow. Right now, I just want sleep. And so do the kids. She's not here."

He scanned the room a final time, checking for the reassuring rise and fall of his children's chests before he turned out their bedroom light. "You're right."

They kept their hands laced as they moved along the hallway, then Louise pulled ahead to collapse back into their bed. Thomas lingered in the hallway to turn out the light, feeling the familiar pull of anxiety in his chest as darkness surrounded him.

Louise had already thrown the blankets back over herself, and

Thomas moved to follow her but stopped on the room's threshold. He stared toward the patch of darkness hiding the stairs. It was empty, but he could have sworn, for a fraction of a second, he'd seen the glint of two eyes.

CHAPTER 2

April 2015

"EIGHT PICTURES OF A rock." Guy held up the stack of photos for his mother to see. "No location or date listed. Bin 'em?"

"Oh…" Heather nudged her glasses farther up her nose. "Those might be significant to someone. We'd better keep those."

Late-afternoon sunshine poured through the attic's windows to bathe Guy and his mother and heat the space a few degrees above what would have been comfortable. Guy crouched on the dusty floorboards, the contents of a cardboard box scattered over the floor in front of him. He drummed his fingers along the edges of the pictures. "Mum, we're the last in our family tree. If they're not significant for you, no one's going to want them."

"I suppose you're right. It's just such a shame to throw out perfectly good pictures..."

Guy raised his eyebrows.

Heather cleared her throat. "Why don't we put them in the 'maybe' box?"

Guy sighed and walked past the nearly empty "throw out" box to place the pictures on top of the overflowing "maybe" carton. When his mother had said the attic didn't need cleaning, he'd assumed she'd forgotten how cluttered the space was. But after two hours of sifting through the leaning towers of filing papers, long-forgotten mementos, and badly broken furniture that "just needs a new coat of paint," he was starting to suspect his mother was secretly a hoarder.

This was meant to be a way to pay her back. Guy returned to the carton and began sorting through thirty-year-old tax returns. *All I'm doing is shifting things from one side of the room to the other. It's not going to help her at all.*

"This is cute! Do you remember this?" Heather straightened and wiggled a stuffed lion toy at Guy. "What did you call it again?"

Guy had to chuckle. "Tiger. I was neither a creative nor smart child."

"I thought it was cute." Heather beamed as she patted the lion's threadbare mane. "Did you want to keep it in your room? It's so stark and bare in there. It might be nice to move some of your old furniture back in."

The familiar sting of failure soured Guy's stomach, but he kept his smile in place. "Thanks, but I like it the way it is."

"Oh, well, if you're sure… Tiger and his friends will be waiting up here if you ever need them." Heather placed the stuffed toy back into the box and resealed it.

Guy watched her move on to a folded stack of hand-knitted sweaters and waited until her back was turned before he let his smile drop.

She didn't deserve to see him discontented. She'd been the only person on his side after what had happened to Savannah. She'd let him move back into her home, fed him, clothed him, and loved him like only a mother could. It was the kind of debt he didn't think he would ever be able to pay back—and it was increasing every week. Heather's pension wasn't designed to feed two people, and Guy's ever-rising stack of rejected job applications wouldn't pay the bills.

Burning anger rose in his throat, but he swallowed it and pushed it back down to where he kept it locked in the small, acorn-sized space in his chest. Anger had gotten him into this mess, and it wouldn't do a thing to get him out.

A large, heavy stack of papers was nestled under the receipts. Guy fished it out, anticipating a tax return or possibly an annual report, and blinked at the dusty cover sheet. He saw an attorney's logo, his mother's name, and an address in large bold letters: 189 Greenhaven Street, Faulconbridge.

"Mum?" He flipped to the second page. "Do you know what this is?"

Heather had unfolded a gnarled maroon sweater with an off-center pink heart and only spared Guy a glance before returning to admire the monstrosity. "Oh, I don't know, dear. Your father used to manage the paperwork."

Incredulity and a small, burning kernel of hope were growing inside Guy as he continued to read. "Mum, this says it's the deed to a house. In your name."

"Oh, that would be for this house, I suppose." Heather refolded the sweater and dug deeper into the box. "Here's a lovely blue top, Guy. It would bring out your eyes."

Guy licked at dry lips. The papers in his hands bore an address located hours away from them. "They're not for this place. It's for a building somewhere in Faulconbridge. Signed over to you in 1985. You must have been young then—"

"Oh!" Realization lit Heather's eyes, and she lowered the blue sweater. "That was the year my father died. He left everything to me. Yes, I think I can remember something about a house now…"

"You're kidding." Guy tried not to gawk. "You've owned a house most of your adult life…and you *forgot?*"

She picked a thread off the sweater. "Well…when my father died, we were still living in his house and didn't really need a second one. I was so young back then, and it was all a rush of funerals and changing accounts and trying to help my mother through her grief. I guess I planned to do something about it eventually, but…" She chuckled. "Yes, I forgot."

Guy's throat had constricted, and he struggled to speak as he turned the pages. "Mum, do you know what this means? We own land. It's talking about nearly two acres of property here, and there's a house on it, too. That's going to be valuable."

"Do you really think so?" She blinked through her thick lenses. "It's got to be a bit old by now, surely?"

Guy rose and wrapped an arm around Heather's shoulders, squeezing her tightly. "I bet it would be worth a fair bit just for the acreage. And if the house is salvageable…"

"What a nice surprise!" Heather patted Guy's shoulder with one hand as she held up the blue sweater in the other. "You know, this really would suit you."

"I'm sure it would." Guy laughed and let go of his mother so that he could run a hand through his hair. "But this house. This could mean—we could—"

Heather beamed up at him. "It's nice to see you so excited over something. You've been down since Sav—since moving back in. Why don't you have that house, if it cheers you up."

Guy shook his head incredulously. *She really doesn't understand what this might mean for us. Money to pay off her home. Or…* Tingling excitement made goose bumps pop up over his arms. *It might even let us move to a new town. One where I'm not known. One where I can get a job. We could both get our lives back on track.*

"I want to have a look at it." Guy ran his thumb over the address on the top sheet. "I'll drive out as soon as we're done here."

"Yes, I'd say we're just about finished." Heather gave a pleased nod toward the mountains of unidentified clutter. "We've had a poke through and found a few things to clear out, but it's pretty tidy, all told."

"If you say so, Mum." Guy might have been tempted to protest if the abandoned property hadn't been whispering to him.

He picked up the "maybe" box and balanced it on his hip as he prepared to take it to the bins.

"Oh, don't throw those out! I think I'd like to keep them after all."

Guy sighed. Heather knit her fingers together and gave him a hopeful smile—one he returned.

It's her attic. If she's happy with it the way it is... "Sure. Where do you want me to put them?"

"Over by the mannequin, honey. Now go on, you can get out of my hair for a bit. I'll cook your favorite pasta for dinner."

"Love you, Mum." He pecked her cheek on the way past, dropped the box off, and moved to the attic's entrance.

I've spent so many disturbed nights dreaming about a fresh start. And all the while it was hidden within twenty meters of where I slept. Guy clutched the papers close to his chest as he bounded down the stairs and snagged his car keys off the hook by the door. *Fancy that.*

CHAPTER 3

WHERE'S THE DRIVEWAY?

Guy looked from the papers in his pickup truck's passenger seat to the cloistering woods surrounding the long, rural road. He had passed the last driveway nearly ten minutes before. Potholes jolted him, and bare branches scraped at the truck's sides. Paranoia had started to set in, and he was asking himself if the house even existed. No one he knew had laid eyes on it; he prayed the property hadn't been swallowed up by the forest during its neglect or condemned and razed by the government for being a health hazard.

Dull metal stood out among the muted greens and browns of the forest. Guy slowed his car as he neared it and shuffled forward in his seat. The shape must have once been a wrought-iron gate. The rusted structure was built a little higher than a man stood, but age hadn't been kind to it. One side of the gate had broken free of its hinges and hung at an angle, supported only by a gnarled tree branch and the chains linking it to its twin.

Guy jumped out of his truck but left the door open. He had to climb through brambles and vines that snagged his boots to reach the metal. Thick flakes peeled off where rust had eaten away at the structure, and a crumbling stone fence ran into the woods on either side. Guy tugged vines away from the plaque across the gate's front to read the words there. *189: Rookward House.*

The trees overhead were too old and dense to let much light through, and Guy shivered in the cooling breeze. He peered through the gate, trying to see past the leaves, but if there was a house there, the foliage shielded it perfectly.

If this really is ours, I can't get in trouble for damaging it, can I? Guy planted one hand on the stone fence and put his boot to the upright half of the gate. When he applied pressure, the metal screeched. Two solid kicks had it bowing inward, and a third broke the bolts and sent it crashing to the ground.

Weeds grew high, and the woods encroached on either side, but Guy could still see the remnants of a path leading through them. He appraised his pickup truck. *She's a tough girl. She'll handle it.*

Guy jumped back into the driver's seat, turned the vehicle to face the gate, and began creeping it forward. The wheels dug into the ground cover then mounted the collapsed gate. A painful shriek escaped the metal as it was crushed. Guy sat on the edge of his seat, alternately pressing his face to the windshield and the driver's side window to watch his progress. The metal shuddered under his vehicle, sending the vines and weeds trembling. Then the pickup truck dropped off the end of the gate and back onto solid ground.

"Good girl." Guy grinned, patting the dashboard, then increased the speed as his vehicle forced its way into the long-forgotten path.

The crackle of crushed plants and the scrape of branches across already-chipped paint filled the truck. More than once, a sapling blocked the way. Guy eased his car around the larger growths and used his utility knife to cut down the smaller ones. As he pressed farther into the forest the connection with the outside world felt fainter. Birdcalls echoed from the canopy, and occasionally, small animals bounded across the path or disturbed the plants alongside the trail.

It was a long, agonizingly slow drive. Despite the air conditioning Guy started to sweat. He'd brought a water bottle but no food, and the niggling worry that his hardened pickup truck would become stuck grew worse as the ground began to slope downward.

Why would anyone build a house so far from the town? Guy squinted into the dappled patches of light that managed to struggle through the overhead coverage. *Mum didn't inherit the place until twenty years ago, so it must be even older than that... Was it a farm? Or maybe a holiday house on the edge of a river?*

The distance from civilization would make it harder to sell unless it had some natural features to make it attractive to city people wanting a vacation property. But if it had been built near a river, as Guy was starting to worry, the landscape could have changed dramatically in the time it had been abandoned. Rivers ate away at the ground and deposited sand where they had once stood, changing their paths over decades. It was even possible the house had been washed away during a flood or storm. The property would still be worth something without a building on it, but nowhere near as much.

The path took a bend, and Guy pressed a hand against the door to brace himself as the truck tipped into an unseen pothole. He'd been driving for far longer than he'd expected. Concerns that he might have missed the house among the forest began to rise, but then he noticed a gap in the trees ahead.

He gave the truck another burst of power to push it through the gap. It rolled onto comparatively even ground and came to a halt. Dozens of tiny insects flicked out of the long grass it had disturbed.

Rookward House stood ahead of Guy, and he took a deep breath as the heavy anxiety fell away from him.

The building was beautiful. Two stories and made of stone, it had withstood the decaying effects of time with what, at first glance, seemed to be minimal damage. Thick, dark-green vines coiled around the house, completely covering most of the ground floor and climbing as high as the second-floor windows. They strangled the building, but Guy saw no sign of collapse or structural failure.

Despite the vines and mottled discoloration of age, the house had a regal, dignified air. Guessing it held at least twenty rooms, Guy thought it must have been expensive to build. The second-floor windows were tall but narrow, and the dark-slate roof appeared mostly intact. The house was dripping with a dark, mysterious kind of personality that made the suburban houses around where Guy lived feel bland in comparison.

The massive oak tree in the front yard showed signs of dying under the weight of its age; the leaves were thinning, and its bark was deeply furrowed and had absorbed a grim shade of gray. A swing hung from the behemoth. The ropes cut into its branch, creating ridges around where it cinched the tree. The cord was fraying, but the discolored wooden seat still shifted a few inches in the breeze. Even inside the pickup truck, Guy heard a prolonged creak as the stiff ropes flexed.

Guy drummed his fingers on the wheel as he chewed his lip, then he leaped out of the truck to get a closer look at the building. Insects darted away from his boots with muted whirrs as he waded through the thigh-high weeds. A few of the second-floor windows were visible between the vines, and their dark panes promised to hold bountiful secrets.

He circled the building in a wide loop. As they had in the front, vines had grown up the stones, but the stone walls still appeared solid. A couple of black marks dotted the roof where tiles had broken off, but none of the holes was very large.

Sharp pain shot up Guy's toe. He hopped back, muffling a curse, and realized he'd walked into a stone embedded in the dirt. He brushed some of the weeds back and found a stone garden border. Guy's eyebrows rose. Tangled among the weeds were a handful of flowers, obviously descendants of the original planting. *They've been hardy to propagate themselves for so many years.*

Guy moved closer to the house's back door. He could see two shades of wood beneath the choking vines. Wishing he'd thought to bring gloves, Guy grabbed at the plants and tugged. They were tough, but clumps of them came away under his pressure. Guy kept digging until half of the door was visible. It might have been painted a lovely shade of blue before age and grime had discolored it, and a brass handle glinted in the low light.

Thick, ugly wooden boards had been nailed across the door to keep it shut. They'd been made from a cheap material and had obviously stood there for decades. Guy tried pulling on them, hoping they'd rotted enough to come away, but they stuck firm.

He moved back from the door and kept circling the house. A darker patch among the vines caught his eye. He stepped up to it and found a hole in the wall. Vines had grown across and through the space, and it took Guy a moment to realize he was looking at a broken window. The wooden frame had been enveloped by the greenery, but when he looked closer he saw a couple of fragments of glass poking through the thready leaves.

It was too much to hope the building would be completely intact. Guy shimmied as near to the opening as the plants would let him and leaned forward to glimpse inside.

A hunched figure stood in the room's corner. With a gasp, Guy jerked back then pressed a hand to his heart as the shape resolved itself. He'd been startled by a coat hung from the back of a door. The fabric was falling apart; shreds of it hung nearly to the floor, and thick dust had dulled its color. It was sobering to think that it had once belonged to someone living in the building. Someone who had loved Rookward, possibly.

Guy moved forward to see the rest of the space. It was some kind of family room. A couch nestled against the back wall. Its blue-print fabric had rotted into its frame, and the cushions had split, spilling their stuffing. Water had come through the open window and made the floorboards bulge across half of the room. Dark mold spread from the corners to climb the wallpaper, and a sickly smell emanated from the space. Guy pressed one sleeve across his mouth and nose.

A handful of small animals—mice, birds, and what might have been lizards—had found their way into the room and died there. Their bones and matted fur stuck to the floor.

Guy wished he could see farther into the house, but both of the room's doors were closed. He contemplated jumping through the window but resisted the impulse. It wouldn't be easy to get over the glass shards still stuck in the frame. Besides, the sun would set soon; if he wanted to examine the property's insides, he would have to come back another day and bring supplies to get the door open. He didn't think he could wait long, though. The need to see inside the building and explore its rooms dug into him like an itch he couldn't quite reach.

He stepped back from the window and continued around the corner. A tree had collapsed against the side of the house. Judging by the bleached, dried wood, it had come down at least a decade before. Guy had to climb over the fractured trunk to get to the house's front. A few of the house's stones were chipped, but the wall still seemed sound. Guy guessed the tree had only clipped the building on its way down.

This is remarkable. He ran a hand across some of the vines wrapping around the building's corner. *It must have been abandoned for a long time—longer than the twenty years Mum has owned it—but it's in good condition. No graffiti, no sign of vandalism or squatters.* Some parts would need repairing, like the water damage to the floors, but the house wouldn't need to be knocked down. And with the furniture gone, it could be livable again. *I should be able to fix up the worst of the damage in a couple of weeks if I dedicate myself to it. It shouldn't be hard to find a buyer.*

Guy stumbled onto the front porch. Vines had fully overrun it, crisscrossing the space like a giant, living spiderweb, but when he peered through, he caught glimpses of the same boards that had been nailed to the back door. Rather than trying to force his way through to them, he stepped back into the weedy yard to admire the building.

It's large. There's got to be twenty, maybe twenty-five rooms in there. No power, of course, and probably no plumbing. But it's a good house, one that will be valuable when it's cleaned up a bit.

Motion pulled Guy's eyes toward one of the upstairs windows. Vines covered the frame but left the glass clear. Guy could have sworn he saw a woman turn away from the glass and retreat into the shadows. He blinked, and the figure was gone.

That couldn't have been a person. He'd been right around the house—the broken window was the only way in, and the dust on the family room's warped floorboards hadn't been disturbed in a long time. *It must have been the shadows playing over the glass.*

Guy stared at the window for a long moment. When he finally looked away, he shivered. The day was cooling as the sun set, and he needed to start the arduous trip through the overgrown trail if he wanted to be back on the main road before dark.

He slid back into his pickup truck and fit the key into the ignition. For the first time since Savannah's accident, he had a purpose. The Rookward house could be sold as-is, but it would fetch more if the vines were cleared away and at least some basic repairs were done. Guy wasn't licensed, but he was handy and didn't mind hard labor. Working on the house would be a way to pay back at least a part of his mother's kindness. And it would keep him occupied for at least a week or two while more job rejections trickled in.

Guy pointed the pickup truck toward the path leading home. As he eased out of the clearing and into the tangled woods, he gave the house a final parting look in his rearview mirror.

It's strange that the vines grow across the building, but not in the yard or the forest. A thought struck Guy, and he smiled at how absurd it was. *It's almost like they're feeding off the building.*

CHAPTER 4

"I DON'T FEEL GOOD about you staying at that house all by yourself." Heather tried to scoop more pasta onto Guy's plate, even though he'd only half-finished the first serving. "It's so far away."

"Three hours, which is why I'll need to stay there." Guy shoveled more of the dinner into his mouth and chewed quickly before continuing. "If I drive there and back every day, it'll take forever to do the repairs. Never mind the fuel costs."

"Well…" Heather sighed and sat back in her seat opposite Guy. She wasn't happy, and Guy thought he knew why. In her eyes, he'd never grown up. He was still a ten-year-old who needed hugs and cookies when he scraped his knees, and wasn't truly safe away from her watchful eye. He wished there was something he could say to give her comfort.

"I'll keep the first trip short. Two nights, how about that? If everything goes well, I can return for a longer visit."

She gave him a tight-lipped smile and nudged at her pasta without picking any up.

A few white lies wouldn't hurt, would they? "It's a lovely house. There's lots of nature around it, so I'll be getting plenty of fresh air, and it seems really solid and secure. Besides, it's not *that* far to get to the local town." *Only an hour's drive.* "Think of it as a vacation house…one I'm doing a bit of maintenance work on while I'm staying there."

Heather's expression brightened. "Maybe I could stay with you! I'm good at painting."

"You are. But I don't think you'd enjoy it as much as I will." Guy didn't want to tell her just how remote and grimy the building was, so he opted for a half-truth. "There's no running water, so you wouldn't be able to have showers."

She took her glasses off and wrinkled her nose. "But won't you start to smell?"

"Oh, definitely." He scooped more pasta into his mouth and watched his mother fiddle with her glasses, her lips pursed. "What kind of bee's in your bonnet tonight?"

"Nothing."

He leaned forward. "I can see there's something. Go on, tell me. Maybe I can help."

She made a muttering noise in the back of her throat as she put her glasses back and picked up her napkin to fidget with instead. "I did some research into the house while you were away. I'm not sure I want you staying there alone."

Guy lifted his eyebrows. "Research? How?"

"I called my aunt Patty—"

"Mum, Aunt Patty died four years ago."

"Yes, of course she did." The napkin was fraying as she continued to twist it around her fingers. "I forgot when I called, but I spoke to her husband, George, instead. His memory isn't very good these days, but he knew a bit about the house. No one has lived in it since the sixties."

"Huh! It's older than I thought." Guy took another bite of his meal. "Did George have anything else to tell you?"

"No…" She hesitated then spoke a little more forcefully. "No. He'd never been there, of course. Apparently, neither had my father. He inherited it as a young man but left it be. It hasn't been opened since the last family left."

"That's weird. Why didn't he sell it?"

"He never told me, honey. Maybe he couldn't find a buyer. Or maybe he forgot about it, like I did."

Impossible. Grandpa's memory was impeccable. "Or he could have been planning to retire there."

"I suppose so."

Guy chewed on the inside of his cheek. Even that explanation didn't make sense; if his grandfather had been intending to live in the house, it made no sense to abandon it completely. He should have rented it out, or at the very least, visited it a few times a year to keep on top of the maintenance.

He watched his mother for a moment. *She's still hiding something.* "Why don't you want me staying there?"

"Oh, I don't know." The napkin finally tore in half. Heather stared at it for a second then threw it onto her plate. "I suppose I just worry."

"You won't need to this time. I'll take care of myself. It's a solid, sturdy house, and I'll bring plenty of supplies. The whole thing probably won't take more than a few weeks to fix up." *As long as the insides aren't too damaged, at least.*

She rose and carried her plate to the kitchen.

Guy felt a sting of guilt; somehow, unintentionally, he'd upset her. He grabbed his own plate and followed. "Mum?"

She'd stopped by the window overlooking their small backyard, where Guy's swing set, his favorite toy as a child, still dominated the space. Guy pressed a hand to her shoulder.

She laughed, though the sound was faintly choked, and turned the tap on to rinse her plate. "You really want to go, don't you?"

"Well, yeah. I've been cooped up for so long. It'll be good to have some work again—especially if it brings in some money."

Her smile was tight. "Well, as long as you keep yourself safe. You'll be back in a couple of days, right?"

"Two days. Promise."

The turnoff to Rookward House was easier to find since the vegetation leading into it had been crushed. Guy didn't feel safe driving over the gate while his pickup truck was weighed down with supplies, but he'd come prepared. He hopped out of the vehicle, grabbed the rope and hook from the passenger seat, and rounded the truck.

One end of the rope went through the gates, then Guy tied it around the rusted chain that linked them together. When the other end was securely fastened to his bumper, he put the truck in reverse and eased it back. The gates had been tangled by weeds, but they came loose when he applied pressure to the accelerator. He drove ten feet down the lane, the gates creating a horrific noise as they clanged against each other, then got out of the truck to untie them.

He struggled to drag the gates into the brush, where they wouldn't trip up any other cars. If no one cleared them away, they would be enveloped by plants within a few months. Guy knew it was technically littering, but he liked the idea of leaving a monument from the house; the gates would have once been a feature of the street, admired by anyone who passed and teasing the style of house that had been hidden from the public's sight. Now they would be allowed to sleep by the road, never again opening, no longer acting as sentry. They would simply rest.

It's not like me to wax lyrical about a lump of metal. Guy climbed back into his pickup truck and turned it into the now-clear driveway. *Maybe this place is getting to me. All of this untouched greenery is something an eighteenth-century poet would go crazy over.*

The path was smoother since it had been forded once. Even with the back of the pickup truck packed high with supplies and tugging the balance off-center, Guy kept up a quick pace. It only took ten minutes for the trees to thin, then Guy emerged into the clearing.

Rookward House commanded his attention like a king holding court. Except this king had fallen startlingly in his fifty-year exile. The few uncovered second-floor windows seemed to glare down at Guy, judging him, but most had been blinded by cataracts made of vines.

"Don't look so hostile. I'm here to salvage you." Guy was struck by how stupid his words sounded as soon as they left his mouth. Grateful that no one was around to have heard him, he eased the truck around the house, to the back door, where he thought he would have easier access to the building. The vines were lighter there, and he wouldn't have to cut his way through the tangled front porch.

He reversed so that the truck's tarpaulin-covered truck bed faced the back door, then he leaped out and stretched. He unhooked the tarp in one corner, where he'd collected key tools in a bucket. Buying the supplies and equipment to repair Rookward House had taken the lion's share of his savings, and there was still more to get. He'd only packed what he knew he would definitely need. He was saving the rest of his money to cover whatever surprises the building had in store for him.

Guy put on a thick pair of work gloves then retrieved a hammer and a crowbar. As he approached the boarded-over back door, he had to fight to remove the last of the vines from the structure. Using the back of the hammer, he wiggled out as many nails as he could reach.

The boards were spongy with slow rot but stubborn. He had to alternate between worming nails out with the hammer and applying brute force with the crowbar to unfasten their hold on the frame. Several fractured and split, leaving half of themselves behind, but by the time Guy stepped back, sweaty and panting, he'd cleared a path to the door.

After all that, it had better not be locked. Residue from generations of vines had crusted the handle. Guy twisted it and grinned as it turned. The latch grated against the strike plate, sending up a mournful wail. Guy forced it open with his shoulder. A rush of stale air washed over him. It smelled like old paper, mold, and decay and held the sticky tang of rotting vegetation.

Inside was unexpectedly dark. The vines were effective at strangling out nearly every trace of sun, and Guy squinted to see into the room. A large, old-fashioned fridge opposite told him he was in the kitchen. Guy nudged the door open as far as it would go and stepped farther into the space to let the light in.

A chopping board and knife sat on the counter beside the sink. A dark, raised stain in the center of the board made Guy think some kind of food had been left to rot on it. The knife still appeared sharp.

Outdated cups, cutlery, and saucers lay in a pile in the sink. They were all stained with muted brown and gray patches, and two of the plates were broken. Guy wondered if the plates had smashed when they were thrown into the sink or whether time had cracked them. One of the teacups held a smudge of red at its top. He leaned closer and recognized a lipstick smear.

A man's coat in the family room, lipstick on the cup, and a swing

29

in the front yard. A couple lived here, then. How many children did they have? And why did they leave so suddenly?

Guy tried to think back to whether there had been any war threats or natural disasters in the area during the sixties, but he couldn't recall any. He supposed anything might have happened to force them out—a sudden illness, a forest fire, or a fatal car accident. It was a shame they hadn't come back; it meant more work to clear out the old furniture.

Still—it's a free house. Not like I can complain.

Guy put his hammer and crowbar on the counter and, tucking the gloves in his pocket, moved to the closest doorway. It opened into a dining room; a family-sized table took up much of the space. Six chairs surrounded it, with one of the chairs pulled out as though its owner had only just left the room. They were barely visible in the refracted light from the kitchen, but the wood shone, even with four decades of dust over it. The furniture was a good quality, though, and a bit of restorative work would make it sellable. Guy circled the table, opened the door at its end, and found a familiar tableau.

He'd stepped into the family room. The tattered coat swirled away from him as the door opened, and little dust eddies skittered over the floor in the light from the broken window. The vines had not only come through the opening, but also twisted over most of the wall. The floorboards bulged where water had warped them, and the mold was thicker and more widespread than Guy had first estimated. He covered his mouth and nose with his sleeve then stepped back and shut the door again.

That'll be a nightmare to fix up. Hopefully, there aren't any other rooms like it.

The dining room's second door led into a foyer. When he squinted, Guy thought he could see the front entry at its end. Low light came down the stairs that had been built into the hallway's side, and multiple other doorways led deeper into the house. Guy paced along the crumbling runner toward the front door then stopped and turned toward the stairs. A low, grating creak came from the second floor as one of its doors drifted open.

CHAPTER 5

"HELLO?"

As soon as Guy spoke, he felt foolish. Of course there wasn't anyone in the house; a door must have been left open.

A tiny thorn of unease niggled at him. *It's a stubborn set of hinges to still be working after all of this time.*

He shifted to face the staircase directly. Even though the upper floor held more light, he couldn't see much from his angle.

I need to have a look around the second floor, anyway. He swallowed and trusted the first step with his weight. It flexed but held. *Why not now?*

The creak echoed through the house again, slower and seeming thoughtful. Guy rested his fingertips on the banister. The dust was thick and tacky. Pictures hung on the wall, but they were impossible to make out through the gloom.

An upstairs window must have been left open to create a breeze. I can only hope it hasn't let water in like in the family room.

Guy took another careful step. The sound around him was magnified, as though he were in an echo chamber. Each breath rang in his ears, and his pumping heart was like a drum.

Light and shadows played across the second floor's white plaster ceiling. One of the shadows was moving, almost like…

Like a pacing figure. Guy stopped halfway up the stairs. Just a few more steps would let him see down the hall and find what was causing the shifting shadow, but the thorny anxiety told him he would be safer if he backed away.

You're being ridiculous. The second floor was deathly silent. His leg felt like lead as he lifted it. *You're alone here. You've got to be. Right?*

Another step, then another, and finally, he had a clear view of the hall. The space held only crumbling wallpaper and open doors. Guy released his tension in a laugh. The foolish feeling intensified.

The door creaked for a third time. The sound came from beyond where the hallway turned a corner, leading to the back of the house. Guy licked dry lips and flexed his shoulders before stepping forward.

The air was cleaner on the second floor, though the tang of organic decay still filled Guy's nose and coated his tongue. The wallpaper was crumpling away in thick strips as moisture loosened its glue. Guy felt some of the wooden boards that lurked behind; they were rough to the touch, which meant they would need sanding, but had been made from a good wood. He thought it might be a feature of the home once the ugly off-white paper with brown stripes was removed.

Patches of the runner's thread came out of its base as Guy's boots scuffed over it. Parts appeared to have been consumed by moths. Dust rose with every step he took, and the particles hung in the air for a long time, stinging Guy's eyes and nose.

He reached the end of the hallway and looked around the bend. The four doors down that section were all closed, and the lack of visibility was striking. A small amount of light struggled through the grime and vines covering the window at the end of the hall, but it wasn't enough to dispel the heavy shadows. They seemed almost human as they clustered, hunched and resentful, in the corners.

If the doors are all closed, where did the noise come from?

Guy's throat was painfully tight. He promised himself it was only from the dust's irritation as he stepped toward the closest door and tried its handle. It was stuck tight, and he had to fight it to get it to open. Inside was a small homey room with walls painted a muted shade of yellow. A sewing machine occupied the only table, and swatches of fabric were pinned to a board nailed to the wall. Part of a gingham dress hung over the back of the chair. Guy picked it up and shook off some of the dust. It was small—a child's dress.

So they had a daughter. How old was she? He held the dress up to the weak light. *Four, maybe? Or five?*

He replaced the dress and turned back to the hallway, only to find the door closed. Guy blinked. *I didn't hear it shut.*

The bronze handle felt oddly cool as he twisted it. The hinges complained as it opened, and Guy, feeling as though he'd lost his balance, retreated to the hallway.

He left the door ajar and stepped back to watch it. Seconds ticked by. Guy's palms itched, and he rubbed them against his jeans. The door didn't even shift a millimeter. Pressure, hot and fierce, built in Guy's chest, burning his insides.

Move, damn you. Show me you're the culprit.

A pulse throbbed in his throat. The heat was growing unbearable, consuming him. His mind shut down. His vision fizzled into black.

He smashed his fist into the door. It slammed closed with a crash that reverberated through the building and seemed to hang in the air even after the echoes died away.

Flashes of white burst through the darkness consuming his vision. He bent over, hands clasped on his knees, and waited for the molten lava filling his insides to cool. It didn't take long.

I thought I was better. Guy opened his eyes. His vision was distorted, like a reflection in a funhouse mirror, but it quickly resolved. He lifted his shaking hands. *Damn it, Guy, what's wrong with you?*

He ran his palms over his face. His eyes stung, but he refused to let any tears escape, even as bitter memories tried to claw their way out of storage. Guy deliberately shut down that part of his mind, drew a quick breath into a too-tight chest, and forced himself to open the next door to give his mind a reprieve.

The space had fewer signs of habitation than the others.

Depressions in the carpet suggested furniture had once filled the area, but only two closed crates and an open closet remained.

Guy tried to visualize what the space might have been. The four indents in the carpet were too close together for a bed... unless it was a child's bed. He blinked, and the room's layout suddenly made sense. It had once belonged to a child—probably the girl whose incomplete dress lay in the sewing room, judging by the faded lavender tint to the curtains.

How come they packed up this room but not the others? Guy approached the closet. A row of rusted coat hangers without clothes hung from the bar. He nudged one of the open doors. It creaked as it shifted. *Looks like I found the source of the sounds, at least. Thank goodness not enough rain came through the window to damage the room—*

The window was closed. Guy frowned and brushed back the curtains to check around the edges. Two dead flies decorated the sill, but the glass was jammed shut.

Then where did the breeze come from?

Guy chewed his lower lip as he stepped away from the window. He gave the closet a final wary glare then tried to lock its door. The wood clicked home but drifted open again as soon as he removed his hand. Guy checked the latch and discovered its metal had been bent. He scanned the space then grabbed one of the closed crates and dragged it in front of the door.

Just in case.

The angle of the light coming through the windows told him the day was progressing quickly. It was easy to lose track of time in the cloistered, surreal house, and Guy was itching to start on his work. He retreated from the abandoned bedroom and tried the next two doors down the hallway. One led into a bathroom with grimy white-tiled walls and stains painted down the sink, toilet, and shower. The other opened into what might have been an office. It held only a wooden chair and empty table. Guy eyed the clear wooden floor. *It might make a good place to sleep tonight.*

His original plan had been to spend the night in the pickup truck's bed, but that would mean being exposed to the weather and morning dew. A space inside the house would be much more comfortable, and the office didn't have any rotted carpet or fabric furniture to clean out. It would be easy to set up his sleeping bag there.

Guy retraced the path around the bend in the hallway. He hadn't explored inside any of the doors in the first section but left them for later. The niggling thorn of unease wouldn't stop digging into him, and he was starving for the clean air of outside. He started down the stairs to the ground floor but stopped at the halfway point and turned. The echoes of a slow, low creak filled his ears. He stared up at the second floor, lips squeezed together, then continued backing down the stairs.

It wasn't the closet, then. I've missed another door somewhere in this house. Or maybe an animal found its way into the ceiling. Either way, I'll deal with it later.

As he reached the foyer, Guy became acutely aware of how dim the lower rooms were. The house was starved of both light and oxygen. That gave him a purpose, at least: clearing the windows.

Guy wove his way back through the dining room and into the kitchen, where the open door offered freedom. A cool breeze brushed over him as he stepped outside. It felt like shedding a heavy, dusty winter cloak, and Guy was glad he wouldn't have to return indoors immediately.

He unhooked the other corner of the pickup truck's tarp and dug through his tools to find shears and a large basin. After tossing them onto the ground beside the kitchen's window, Guy started the slow, arduous task of tearing the vines off the house.

Grime and dead insects rained over his head as he yanked at the plant. Sap bled out of the torn stems, staining the gloves and sending tiny sprinkles of the sticky syrup over his face and arms. And yet, despite the dirt, Guy found the work gratifying. Once he'd loosened their hold, the vines came off the building in large clumps. It was cathartic.

It took ten minutes to fill the tub, creating a cleared patch of wall a meter wide and two meters high. The vines had left a black rotting residue that stained the stones and glass. Guy could wash the windows, but he guessed the color would never come out of the stones. He crossed his fingers that, once the whole house was cleared, the effect would be artistic rather than repulsive.

He grabbed one of the tub's handles and began dragging it toward the woods' edge. The clearing must have been larger at one time, but trees and shrubs had gradually filled in the space. The path became too crowded to maneuver the tub after forty feet, so Guy dumped the vines there and returned to the house.

Working along the wall sequentially would have taken days,

so Guy focused on finding windows. They weren't always visible behind the plants, but it didn't take too much guesswork to locate them—the vines always formed a little ridge around the sill and indented for the glass.

As he worked around the building, Guy peered through the windows, catching glimpses of rooms he hadn't yet visited. He discovered a small library, its shelves mostly empty and its overstuffed couches sagging to the ground. Then a laundry with a small window set so high that he had to stretch to reach the top. Finally, near the front of the house, he began working on the vines over a large window, which he could only assume opened into the dining room. The patch covering the lower-left pane came away and revealed an odd gray shape pressed to the other side of the glass. Guy hadn't taken a close look at the room, but he thought he remembered it being mostly clear of clutter. He kept tugging. A large swath of the vine broke off with a thick crackling noise, raining grime over Guy's forearm and face. He blinked to clear away the grime. A woman stared at him through the window.

CHAPTER 6

THE SPLAYED FINGERS PRESSED to the glass were the only clear part of the stranger. They were grayed and strangely mottled, like a sea creature left in the sun for too long. From the fingers, a bare arm stretched away from the glass, growing less distinct until it faded into a blurry torso and face. Guy had the impression of thin lips, high cheekbones, and long hair, then the figure stepped back from the window, fading into the shadows like a ship in a sea of fog.

A choked cry escaped Guy. He staggered away from the window, heart in throat, and reflexively raised his handful of vines as a shield.

Without his body to block the sunlight through the window, the room's interior was clearer. He could see the table with its chair pulled out, the china cabinet, and the two closed doors. There was no sign of the woman.

Guy swallowed around the lump in his throat. He threw the vines to the ground and half walked, half jogged toward the back door. Passing his pickup truck, he seized a hammer from among the tools that filled the back. He held it ahead of himself as he stepped up to the open kitchen door. "Hello!"

Even as he spoke, he knew he wouldn't get a response. His skin crawled, and his heart leaped as he crept over the kitchen's threshold. Floating flecks of dust glowed in the light coming through the window, and their motion kept catching in the corners of his eyes. He inhaled through his mouth and rolled his feet to muffle the noise as he shifted toward the door to the dining room.

The handle screeched as he turned it, making Guy flinch. He bumped the door open with his foot, hammer held above his head just in case, but the space beyond was still empty.

She can't have escaped through the kitchen, or I would have seen her when I went to the pickup truck. That means she went…where? Into the family room? Up the stairs?

Guy tried the door to the family room first. The space remained intact, the way he'd last seen it—fluffs of decayed mouse fur on the floor, mold creeping over the walls, and vines strangling the window. The gap between the plants was too small for a human to fit through without disturbing the foliage. Guy gave the room a fleeting scan before closing the door again.

He went to the door leading to the hallway and bent his ear close to the wood to listen. A bird called out in the distance. Guy's heartbeat thundered. For a moment, no other noises reached his ears. Then a floorboard groaned.

Guy threw open the door. It banged against the wall and rebounded, the wood shivering from the impact. The space beyond was empty.

I didn't imagine it…did I? The lump in Guy's throat had grown painful. He stepped into the foyer and looked in both directions. *I'm not crazy, and I'm not delusional. If someone's in my house, I've got to make them leave.*

The mysterious door upstairs groaned closed again. A dreadful weariness coursed through Guy, making his limbs feel heavy. He approached the stairs, touched the dusty banister, and began to climb.

The old boards were noisy beneath his feet, even though he tried to stay to the stair's edge. Dust stirred up during his earlier exploration still hung in the air. He wondered how long it would take to fully settle. Hours? Days? The hallway came into view in increments but remained empty.

At the top of the stairs, Guy stopped to listen. The upper floor felt eerily quiet. He held his breath, ears straining, then flinched as the door to his left moved.

The hinges groaned as they shifted. The door drew inward, as though inviting Guy into the room. He tightened his grip on the hammer and approached.

The double bed, sheets neatly made and pillows squared, suggested he'd found the master bedroom. It was a bizarre sight; the bed was impeccably tidy, except for the muffling layer of dust. The center of the mattress sagged sadly, and the once-white pillowcases were an unappealing yellow.

The room was empty, but he'd finally located the source of the shifting door. *Odd that I didn't see it move the first time I stood on the landing. Maybe I was facing the wrong direction?*

He lowered the hammer. The longer the search went on, the more convinced he felt that he wouldn't find anyone. The figure at the window had seemed so vivid at the time, but doubt had started to prick holes in the memory. *Am I really, truly sure it was a woman, and not an illusion? Maybe I saw my own reflection. Shadows from the trees could have given the impression of long hair. Because it's impossible for someone else to be in the house. It's got to be impossible.*

The large window held a view of the woods behind the house. Only a handful of straggly vines blocked the glass, but they couldn't reach more than halfway up. Guy approached the window.

There was no sign of humanity in any direction. No lights, no smoke, no break in the carpet of green growing over the hills surrounding him. He'd never felt so isolated in his life.

There isn't anyone in Rookward. There couldn't be, because there was no running water and no food. No one would survive there without supplies, and to bring any quantity of supplies, a car would have been necessary, and Guy's truck was the only vehicle on the property. The thought wasn't as reassuring as he would have liked it to be.

He rubbed at the hairs that had risen over the back of his arms. A bird flitted through the trees then took off in a flurry of wings and shrieks. Something about the woods—their expansiveness, their density, or their coloring—made Guy's pulse quicken. He tucked the hammer into his back pocket and stepped away from the window.

A dull-blue baby monitor sat on the bedside table. The speaker was crusted over, and the paint was chipped, but it looked similar to the baby monitors Guy had seen in the window of the local dollar store. He imagined what it would have been like to buy one with Savannah, picking out their favorite color, reading the instruction manual together. A sickening, miserable ache settled in his chest, and suddenly, he wanted nothing more than to escape the bedroom.

Guy drew in a series of harsh gasps in the hallway. His hands were shaking, and his head ached. He no longer cared about what he thought he'd seen in the window; he just wanted some kind of action that would give his mind a reprieve from itself. The vines offered that in bountiful measure. He stumbled down the stairs, knocked the dining room chair further askew as he passed it, and stalked around the outside of the building until he found the basin. Then he attacked the vines near the kitchen door, tearing at them, not noticing when flecks of dirt hit his bared teeth or shoots scraped his arms. He abandoned his original plan of working through the windowed sections methodically and grabbed any plant within reaching distance. If the vine grew too thick to pull up at its base, he used the shears to hack through it.

Each time he passed one of the windows, he reflexively set his jaw and narrowed his eyes before tearing the foliage away from it. No phantom faces appeared.

His intensity gradually dulled as he spent his energy. By the time he staggered away from the house, grimy, scratched, and bone-tired, he felt only a foggy, indistinct sadness.

He'd cleared most of the western wall in his frenzy. Some of the plants still clung to the stones beyond his reach, but he suspected they would wither and fall off after a few days without roots. The conquered vines had overflowed his bucket early in the assault and littered the ground in clumps. It would take a few trips to get them into the forest, but Guy's hands were numb, and his arms ached, so he figured that could wait until after he'd rested and eaten.

He stripped off the gloves and flexed his fingers. They were red but the only part of him that hadn't been splattered with sap and grime. He glanced toward the driveway, where a hot shower and comforting hug were just a few hours away. He could get into his pickup truck and not have to worry about what he'd seen—or *thought* he'd seen—ever again.

No, you committed to this. Don't flake.

Guy snorted and went back to the truck. He dragged out one of the large jugs of water he'd brought. If he'd possessed the energy and motivation, he could have lit a fire and figured out a way to heat the water, but it seemed like too much effort for such a small luxury. He stripped and, with soap from his toiletries bag and cupfuls of water sloshed out of the jug, did his best to clean himself.

There's no one inside the house. He scrubbed suds into his hair and tried to ignore the weight of the unease that had settled onto his back. *There can't be. It's an old house, and the atmosphere is making your mind think it sees things that aren't real. You won't help anything by worrying about it, so put it out of your mind. Do your job.*

By the time he changed into a fresh set of clothes the jug was empty, he was shivering, and he felt nowhere near as clean as he would have liked. The sap was stubborn and probably wouldn't fully peel off without an exfoliating scrub. In spite of that, his mood had lifted, and he'd regained at least part of his earlier enthusiasm. Something about washing in the outdoors made him feel stronger and bolder.

Status check. We've got one quarter of the building clear of vines. That should let some light into those rooms, at least. Which means I can set up a bit of a base and start stripping the house's guts out.

He hopped from one foot to the other in an effort to warm himself. The house loomed over him, its black windows ever watchful, and he half wished he could stay outside and continue attacking the vines. But there was a lot to do before the sun set. At the very least, he needed to set up a place to sleep and develop a plan for clearing out the damaged furniture.

Procrastinating never achieved anything. Get moving.

Guy set his shoulders, collected armfuls of equipment from the pickup truck's back, and stepped through the kitchen door.

CHAPTER 7

THE HOUSE LOOKED WHOLLY different with light. As Guy looped through the dining room, his sleeping bag and bucket of supplies in one arm and spare blankets slung over his shoulder, he could finally see the fruit-patterned plates in the china cabinet and the chips and scratches on the table. He stopped in the foyer to listen, but the only noises were deep, heavy creaks from the aged wood shifting as the sun warmed it.

All of the downstairs rooms were filled with decaying furniture, which meant the cleanest place to sleep would be the empty upstairs room he'd found earlier. Guy began climbing the stairs. The family portraits on the walls were finally visible, and he stopped to study his predecessors.

They showed a family of five: a brown-haired, middle-aged man sat in the center of a couch, one arm draped over his wife's shoulders. She was tall and thin, and a small smile curled her lips. Sat on either side of them were a boy, a girl, and a toddler.

Although the arrangement was banal, the picture made Guy's skin crawl for reasons he couldn't fully articulate. There was something fundamentally, thoroughly wrong with it. The husband's eyes didn't quite meet the camera. The children weren't smiling. Although the man's arm rested over his wife's shoulders, the fingers were lifted away from her skin, as though he were reluctant to properly hold her. And even disguised by the picture's warped colors, the family was unusually pale, as though they never left the house.

He leaned away from the photographs and continued up the stairs. The more he explored the house, the more he believed that there was something strange about the family that had once owned it. *Maybe they belonged to some kind of fundamentalist cult?* That would explain why their home was so remote. It might also provide a reason for their sudden departure if they were expecting the end of times or had been called away by their cult leader.

They must have been related to us somehow for Grandpa to inherit their home. I wonder if he knew them? Did he ever visit here as a child? Was there a reason he never used this place?

Guy's curiosity was piqued. He couldn't afford to spend weeks picking through the building for clues, but he intended to keep his eyes open. With luck, he might find hints during the cleaning to tell him what had happened.

He reached the top of the stairs and started toward the empty room at the other end of the hallway. As he passed the doors he hadn't opened yet, he stopped to look inside them. The children's bedroom was right next to the master bedroom. Two beds and a crib had been crammed into the space, and the other half of the baby monitor hung from the end of the crib. That puzzled Guy; the house was easily large enough for each of the children to have a room—and there was evidence that they had, at one point—but they'd all been crowded into the one space.

Almost like they were afraid to sleep alone.

Guy shivered and kept moving. He found a bathroom and tested the tap. The pipes were bone dry, which didn't surprise him. If the water had been shut off, the solution might be as simple as getting it reconnected, but because it was so far from other houses, Rookward was more likely to run on well water. In that case, if the tap wasn't functional, the fault was in the pipes. If he couldn't find the problem and fix it himself, he would either have to pay a plumber or sell the house as-is and take a hit on the profit.

Past the bathroom was another mostly empty room with indents on the carpet where a bed had once sat. *Was it the children's choice to move in together, or the parents?* Either explanation was strange. He hitched the sleeping bag a little higher under his arm and turned the hallway's corner.

The final room, which held only a table and a chair, was a welcome relief from the rest of the building. There was no evidence of the previous family to unnerve or depress him. Two well-sized windows overlooked the woods and let in a healthy level of light. The only thing about the room Guy didn't like was how far he needed to travel to get outside. The idea of racing along the hallway, trying to reach the kitchen door but having to pass through virtually the entire house, flashed through Guy's mind. He dismissed it after a moment of hesitation. The only plausible threat to his safety was a house fire, and he was too careful to start one by accident.

Guy dropped the bucket and snagged a dust cloth out of it. He wiped down the table before putting his bedding there, then he set to work sweeping out the rest of the room. He was glad the family had chosen to leave the wooden floorboards instead of covering them with carpet; it made his job infinitely easier. Setting up his bedroom took no more than a couple of minutes. He unrolled the sleeping bag on top of a layer of blankets and tossed the pillow on top.

An odd crackling noise made him turn toward the door. The sound faded after a second, leaving Guy frowning. If he hadn't known it was impossible, he would have thought he'd heard distorted voices coming through the baby monitor.

It's probably branches dragging across the stones. Or maybe some kind of animal living in the attic. I'll have to check up there before I finish working on the building.

He had little time before nightfall would make work too difficult, so Guy jogged back downstairs and went to unpack the truck. He dragged the remaining jugs of water and crates of food into the dining room and arranged them on the table. Then he collected changes of clothes, flashlights, and his radio before refastening the tarp over the work tools to protect them from the damp night air.

A crimson sunset painted the tops of the trees as Guy ate a muesli bar and wandered through the house's lower level. A guest room stood opposite the stairs, and he admired the once-grand furniture there. Even though time had stained the chair covers yellow and left dust across the surfaces, Guy had the impression the room had never seen much use, even when the house was inhabited.

An ornate wooden clock stood on the fireplace's mantelpiece. It had died at 12:15. Guy's own phone wouldn't last long without any power source, so he used it to adjust the clock's time then wound it up. A soft *tk-tk-tk* filled the room as the second hand advanced around the dial. Guy grinned at it. It was a beautiful clock—as long as it could keep the time, he would take it home and give it to his mother.

He opened his phone, intending to call Heather, but it didn't have any service bars. Guy held the mobile above his head, hoping a few bars would appear, but he eventually had to turn it off and tuck it back into his pocket. He was on a budget plan, and the service was dodgy on a good day, so it wasn't much of a surprise that the isolation rendered it useless.

He placed his radio next to the clock and turned it on. Static flooded the room as Guy hunted for a station. There wasn't much available at Rookward, so he settled on one that played classics. Screeching violins filled the air, and Guy poked his tongue out in disdain, but he preferred it to the silence.

Guy retrieved a pen and notepad from the dining room and began making a list of supplies he still needed to buy. Most of his money would have to go toward fixing the family room. Glass was expensive, and he would probably have to strip the walls and floor to get rid of the mold. But he also wrote down any other equipment and materials he hadn't packed into the truck, including a weed cutter and paint for the walls.

If I max my credit card, I should have enough to pay for everything. Just barely. Let's hope the house doesn't have any other surprises for me.

The song floating out of the guest room faltered then broke. A strange, echoing stillness replaced it. Frowning, Guy lowered his notepad. The radio crackled, and the song resumed for no more than two seconds before dying again.

He pocketed the paper and stepped into the guest room. Streaks of thin, insipid light coming through the grimy window distorted the room's colors, turning the area into a nightmarish scape of reds and burnt golds.

Almost as though it could feel him staring at it, the radio released a burst of static. Something was audible through the crackles. Guy stepped closer, his dry tongue sticking to the roof of his mouth. *It's like someone breathing…*

He pushed the volume up. The rasping, grating noise grew clearer, encapsulated in static but strangely distinct.

Did I accidentally pick up a private broadcast? Did the announcer leave the microphone on without realizing?

The breaths were quick, almost frantic. He raised the volume again, until its echoes filled the room, and he caught the muffled sound of footsteps underneath the inhalations.

Guy was struck by a sudden, disorienting sensation that the source came from behind him. The steps fell on the carpet, creating a muted crunch of crushed fibers. The breathing was so close that he expected to feel the exhales across the back of his neck…

He turned. Shadows hung heavy about the room as twilight gave way to night. He was alone, but the sensation of eyes following his movements wouldn't abate. Guy switched off the radio. Somehow, the silence that replaced the static was even worse.

CHAPTER 8

April 1965

THOMAS LEANED AGAINST THE kitchen's doorframe. A vicious wind tugged at the trees, ripping off leaves and bending some of the more supple trunks nearly horizontal. Any late-afternoon sun had been blotted out by clouds. He swept his eyes across the spaces between the trees, back and forward in a constant loop. He knew she was there, even if he couldn't see her. It was an awful feeling to be watched without any way to watch back.

"Thomas?"

He turned to face Louise. She'd entered the kitchen silently and stood by the fridge, her face calm but her arms folded.

The words were out of his mouth before he had a chance to consider whether they were wise. "I'm not delusional."

"I know." She seemed to be trying to sound reassuring, but the undercurrent of uncertainty in her tone left him feeling sick. She licked at her lips and looked away, toward where Thomas could hear his children playing in the family room. "Something's got to change."

"We need to be patient."

"It's been weeks, Thomas. You need to go back to work before you lose your job."

An irrational frustration built in his chest. He knew Louise was trying to be supportive, but she still didn't seem to under-stand the severity of the situation. The old tree by the side of the house scratched at the stones, its dead branches scraping, scraping, scraping... It needled his nerves, making him twitchy and irritable.

He stepped away from the door and lowered his voice, even though there was no way his words could carry to the woods. "Not yet. She can't keep this up much longer. We've just got to hold on a little more, and I'm sure she'll snap."

Louise chewed on her lip. "When was the last time you saw her?"

"What? She's out there right now—"

"But you haven't *seen* her, have you?"

"I can feel her!" The words came out more harshly than he'd intended. Louise's face tightened, and Thomas cleared his throat and lowered his voice. "I can feel her watching me. Constantly." After a beat of silence, he repeated, "I'm not delusional."

Louise exhaled and rubbed at the inner corners of her eyes. She opened her mouth to say more but instead waved a hand and crossed to the family room. Aching frustration tightened Thomas's throat as he watched her go. He knew Louise wanted to believe him, but it was hard for her when Amy kept so well hidden.

And she was right. The bank wouldn't welcome him back if he took too much more time off work.

But what else can I do? He chewed at his too-short thumbnail as he moved back to the window. The eyes were still there, unseen but intense enough to make his skin crawl. He thought she must be smiling.

"Damn it; damn it all." Returning to work would mean leaving his family alone, and that was too risky to even consider. But he'd been away for weeks. Vague excuses about prolonged illness wouldn't carry him much further. For all he knew, it might already be too late; he could step through the bank's doors and face a termination notice.

I could tell them the real reason we spend our days huddled inside our home, but... Picturing Westmeyer's flat, bull-like face, Thomas squeezed his lips together. Westmeyer wouldn't take the news about Amy easily. Thomas and his job would be safer if he kept mute on that quarter.

A branch snapped free from its tree and tumbled across the overgrown lawn. Thomas watched it until it disappeared past the corner of the house. His thumb ached from where he'd gnawed the nail too far.

Louise is right. This wait is killing us.

He pushed away from the window and went into the dining room. The table was large enough for a banquet. Thomas ran his hand over the dark wood and tried not to let the corners of his mouth twitch down. Compared to the cramped apartment he and Louise had stayed in when they had first married, and the barely larger suburban house they'd moved to when Dan and Becca were born, Rookward was a palace. But instead of feeling luxurious, the rooms carried an air of neglect. Furniture that had fit snugly into their old house was dwarfed by the empty space around it. Some days, Thomas felt as though they were staying in a hotel; fragments of their lives were scattered through the building, but they didn't belong, not really.

The tree continued to scratch at the wall. It sounded like a dog begging to be let in. Thomas's fingers itched with the urge to snap the dead branches off.

His attention drifted back to the window and the forest beyond it. Something on the glass caught his notice. Thomas rounded the table and bent over the windowsill to see it more clearly. Letters had been scratched into the bottom-left corner of the glass, just above the frame. They were jagged and every line painfully straight, making Thomas think they had been cut with the sharp corner of a stone: PROMISE.

His fingers trembled when he reached out to touch the words. They were small, small enough that he wouldn't have noticed them if he hadn't been staring at the window. He swallowed and found his mouth painfully dry.

How long have these been here? Did I just not notice them before today, or are they fresh?

An image flashed through his mind: Amy, her dark hair a

mess of tangles about her face, her dark eyes horrifically intent, pressed against the side of their house as she carved her message. Thomas's stomach churned.

He rubbed his thumb over the marks, as though he could erase them, but they'd been cut into the outside of the glass. Amy would have had to write each letter backward so that it was readable from inside. Thomas pulled his hands back and wrapped them around his torso.

The gale seemed to grow fiercer. It whipped at the forest, stripping branches and leaves. Flecks of dirt danced across the lawn and stone-bordered flower garden. Louise had planted fresh plants—poppies and carnations—two days before, but he could no longer see the cheerful reds and golds bobbing in the wind. Thomas squinted, and his breath fogged over the glass as he leaned closer to the window. The flowers had all been cut; only the stems remained. Long and bright green, they poked up like empty flagpoles, but the jewels topping them had been removed. The sight made Thomas's skin crawl. It was like witnessing the aftermath of a beheading.

He turned aside. The blood in his veins was too hot. His scalp itched, and he scratched at it as he paced into the foyer. He'd thought Rookward would be a sanctuary, their safe shelter to keep the hungry tiger out. But it had become a cage instead. The tiger paced around, ever restless, ever watchful, and he was helpless to leave.

Thomas pressed his hands over his ears as he came to a halt in the foyer. The scratching was unbearable. The dead branches never stilled for even a moment but scraped at the house, setting his teeth on edge and mingling with the swing's groans to create an awful, unceasing cacophony.

No…it's not branches. Thomas dropped his hands and looked to the left, toward the foyer's front door. The tree grew by the house's other side, near his bedroom. The incessant scratching was coming from the porch.

His tongue was coated with a tacky, unpleasant flavor as he moved toward the door. His palms itched worse than ever, but he felt incapable of turning away, no matter how much he wanted to.

The foyer's lights didn't reach the front door quite as well as they should have. It left the area in shadows, though a block of thin light came through the rectangular window set at head height. The wood shivered. Thomas tried to tell himself it was the wind, but the scratching was louder.

He reached out and rested his fingertips against the door. It reverberated under his hand, and the shudders echoed through Thomas's limbs and down his spine. His breath was shallow, but his lungs felt too small for anything more. He took another step forward, until his face was at the window. The stippled glass distorted the outside world. He saw a shimmer of dark wood— the porch's supports—and, farther away, the blurred forest being rocked by the gale.

Thomas bent an inch closer, until his nose nearly grazed the glass, as he strained to see into the deep gloom of the porch's corner. He held his breath, but he could no longer hear the scratching.

A hand slammed into the window. Amy's long, bloodless

face appeared beside it, ghosting out of the shadows. Wild eyes fixed on him. Colorless lips stretched into a demented smile. Her wild hair lashed about her face, pulled into disarray by the vicious wind.

Thomas yelped as he jerked back. He reflexively reached for the door's three bolts, but they were all drawn and locked. He stumbled back until he hit the staircase's banister, his heart caught in his throat and beating so fiercely, he thought he might collapse.

Amy's unblinking eyes tracked his every movement, watching him hungrily. Thomas turned and dashed up the stairs, using his hands to aid his ascent and knocking the family portraits askew.

The scratching, scrabbling sound resumed as Amy drew her nails across the wood, wordlessly asking to be let inside.

CHAPTER 9

GUY STARTED AWAKE. HE was freezing cold, but some of the shivers came from the dream that had woken him. He'd been standing in Rookward's foyer, looking for something—or someone—outside. Guy frowned, trying to retain the details of the dream, but they drained away from him before he could grip them.

He rolled over to face the window. The crescent moon fought to pierce the clouds. He rubbed at his blurred eyes and groaned as the muscles protested. *It's been a while since I did so much physical work in one day. On the upside, I'll probably be super buff by the time I'm done with this house.*

The air was freezing. Guy briefly considered running to the truck for the spare set of blankets. He reached for his phone, which he'd left next to his bed, to check the time. Its batteries were already dead. He snorted and put it aside.

It can't be too far to dawn, surely? As soon as the sun comes up, I'll get out the portable stovetop and boil some coffee.

Guy tried to lie still and wait for sleep to reclaim him, but the forgotten dream had left him twitchy. He counted the passing seconds as he watched shadows creep across the ceiling.

A door groaned. He squeezed his lids closed. The sound hung in the air long after it should have, jarring his nerves and making his palms sweat despite the chill.

I shut the master bedroom door. I shut the child's closet. What's making the noise?

A floorboard squeaked. Guy's eyes shot open. He held still, breath frozen in his lungs, as he strained his ears. Silence reigned for a prolonged moment, then a second floorboard flexed, this time closer to his room.

It's just the house moving in the wind. He worried at his lower lip. A scraping, scratching noise came from the hallway, as though someone were running their fingers across the tattered wallpaper.

Guy tasted blood as his tooth nicked the skin. His breathing was unnaturally loud, but he was incapable of quietening it. The scratching noise drew closer, grating at his nerves and chilling his blood, then ceased just outside his room.

Get up! His limbs didn't want to move. *Find a weapon, idiot!*

Guy thrashed his way out of the sleeping bag in a burst of energy. He lunged toward the table, where he'd left the flashlight, the only weighty, solid object in the room. Guy seized it, silently cursing himself for not bringing at least a hammer. He pressed the button, but the light didn't turn on.

No. C'mon! Don't do this!

He'd checked the batteries before loading the flashlight into the pickup truck. *Did it somehow turn on during the drive and drain them?* Guy hit the button several more times, but he remained surrounded by darkness.

The noises in the hallway didn't repeat. Guy considered leaving the door shut—even bracing the chair against the handle to jam it—but that would put him in the worst possible position. He'd left the truck's keys in the dining room. If the stranger found them, they could take the vehicle, leaving Guy stranded at the house without any transportation or phone.

He wasn't a small man, and none of his acquaintances would have described him as meek, but the idea of opening the door terrified him. The sounds had stopped on the threshold, which meant he would have only a split second to assess and respond to whatever waited on the other side—and his only defense came from a broken flashlight and his fists.

As Guy reached for the handle, a new idea flitted through his mind. *What if the being outside isn't human?* He pictured something unnaturally elongated and sightless, its toothy maw stretched wide. Or perhaps the woman he'd seen earlier, her pale skin, still blurred and distorted even without the glass filter, waited with her long, bony fingers stretched toward him. His mind knew it was a fantasy—but at that moment, in the heart of nighttime and isolated in a house that turned his stomach, he couldn't erase the images from his mind.

Do it now, quickly, before you lose your courage.

He twisted the handle and yanked open the door. Its hinges wailed, and Guy flinched as his mind interpreted the noise as a monster's scream.

Darkness enveloped the hallway except for the rectangle where moonlight washed through his open door. Guy hunted through the darkness, straining to pick out any motion or color.

Something crackled and clicked to his right. Guy swiveled toward it, his heart blocking his throat. It took him a second to identify what he'd heard: the baby monitor coming to life.

That's impossible. He stepped out of the room, his instincts begging him to stay put but his mind insisting he had to get the keys. *The batteries would be long dead. There's no way it can still work.*

But what else could it be?

The crackles stuttered into silence then started again, slightly louder. It might have been his imagination hunting for patterns among chaos, but Guy thought he caught the lilt of a word among the static.

He took another step then a third. Each pace took him deeper into the blackness, closer to the source of the disturbance, and he stretched out a hand. The fingers touched the dry, brittle wallpaper. He wanted to cringe away from it, but it was his only guidance that night.

The baby monitor fell back into silence. Guy's fingertips grazed the corner where the hallway turned, and he followed it around. The master bedroom's door stood open. A block of moonlight flowed through.

I closed it…didn't I?

He held the distinct memory of shutting the door, but as he moved nearer, doubt permeated his mind. *What if I only dreamed I shut it?*

As he passed the children's bedroom, the baby monitor came back to life, this time carrying the sounds of his own footsteps. They were badly distorted and thick with interference but clear enough that they couldn't have been anything else. He stopped in front of the master bedroom door and nudged it fully open.

Vivid bloodstains drenched the bed. The liquid ran over the quilt, dribbling to the ground, and spread across the carpet like a halo. In the moonlight, it took on an ethereal sheen, but the smell was unmistakable. It filled Guy's mouth and throat, making his stomach lurch. He grabbed at the door's frame to keep himself on his feet as dizziness roared through him.

The baby monitor on the table beside the bed crackled. A woman's voice spoke through it. The words were muffled but awfully, chillingly serene. "Thomas. Don't leave me, Thomas…"

Guy's vision swam. He staggered backward, and his legs failed, dropping him to the floor. The impact jarred his teeth and sent his head spinning. He lay there for a moment, eyes fixed on the cracked ceiling as he struggled to draw in oxygen, then the world leveled as the roar in his ears faded.

Moving gingerly, Guy raised himself into a sitting position. The smell no longer bothered him. He blinked toward the bedroom. The shadows were thick, but he couldn't see the bloodstains.

"What…"

He'd dropped the flashlight when he fell. He picked it up and, on a chance, pressed the button. A bright circle of light appeared on the wall opposite. Confusion fogged Guy's mind as he blinked at the beam then turned it toward the open door.

The bed was clean, its blue quilt dusty but unstained. The baby monitor beside it stayed quiet. *What the hell just happened?*

Guy rolled onto his knees then slowly got to his feet. They shook, but a dread-filled curiosity made them carry him toward the children's bedroom. He sought out the transmitter attached to the crib's edge and tapped it twice. No noise came from the master bedroom. He dropped the receiver and returned to the hallway to check the room a final time, just in case. The bed, dust-coated and dry, stood where it was supposed to.

Was I sleepwalking? Guy's first instinct was to reject the idea— the experience had seemed too vivid, too *real*—but it made a lot of sense. The footsteps, the baby monitors that worked decades after their batteries must have run out, the nonexistent blood, the voice—there was no way it could have been a real experience. Guy had felt vaguely uneasy ever since arriving at Rookward, and the nerves had combined to make him sleepwalk and served up a nightmare at the same time.

He lowered the flashlight and rubbed at the bridge of his nose. His head still hurt from when he'd fallen, and his heart refused to slow. *I haven't sleepwalked since I was a kid. And even then, I never had dreams during it. Maybe the house is getting to me more than I thought.*

The building was still dark, but when he looked through the

master bedroom's window, the barest hint of light glossed over the top of the trees. *Nautical dawn. That means real dawn isn't too far away.*

He glanced to his right, where the hallway led to his bedroom. Guy didn't think he would be able to sleep again that night. So he turned toward the stairs and let the flashlight's beam guide him to the lower level.

Rookward was beautifully quiet. Not even the ticking of the guest room clock reached him. Guy went into the dining room and found the keys where he'd left them on the table. There was no longer any urgency to leave the house, but he tucked them into his pocket anyway and dug the portable stovetop out of his crate of supplies. He set it up and warmed his fingers by the flames for a moment before filling a saucepan with water and setting it on top to heat.

It's a bad start to the day, but I can't let this demotivate me. Remember why you're here. He squeezed his eyes closed and thought of his mother and her helpless, anxious smile as she tried to help him brainstorm a way out of their financial problems, even though they both knew there was no easy fix. The way she tirelessly cooked his favorite meals in an effort to cheer him up. Her unwavering faith. And the friendships she'd lost because of him.

Heather had moved Guy back into her house after the incident with Savannah, and for a lot of people, that made her guilty by association. Heather pretended not to notice the pitying glances and judgmental sneers from their neighbors when they passed her in the street, but Guy didn't think he could ever forgive them for it. No more than he could forgive himself. Heather had lost her friends because of him. She was the kindest woman he knew; she didn't deserve to be shunned by anyone.

She won't be for much longer. Once we sell Rookward, we can move somewhere no one knows us. I can make her proud again.

Guy dropped his head and let his shoulders slump. The pot boiled, but it took him a long time to take it off the stove.

CHAPTER 10

DAWN WAS BITTERLY COLD. Guy compensated by wearing two layers of clothes. He ate breakfast in the dining room, shivering and hunched over his bowl of dry cereal. Tendrils of mist swirled across the lawn, masking the forest. Something small had been etched into the corner of the glass. Squinting to make out the letters, he realized he already knew what it said.

PROMISE.

Odd. Did I see it yesterday and just forget it was there? He felt like it was somehow connected to his dream, but the memory was too blurred to recall. He shivered and spooned more flakes into his mouth. The extra clothing wasn't doing much to remove the chill, so he decided some high-energy work might help. As soon as he'd finished breakfast and washed up, he unloaded the last of the equipment from the truck and tucked a roll of garbage bags into his pocket.

He went through the house, starting with the kitchen, and put anything organic or decayed into a bag. That included the threadbare rugs and the cloths and fabrics in the cupboards. When a bag was full, he tied it up and threw it into the back of the truck.

The large sofas in the guest room caused him some problems. After trying—and failing—to drag them outside, he settled on using a hatchet to cut them into pieces he could carry. It was easier than he'd expected; the fabric had absorbed moisture and weakened the wood, and the structures mostly broke apart with a few well-aimed hacks. They left a mess of splinters and scraps of fabric scattered across the floor, but the room's carpet would need to be pulled up anyway.

Once the last sofa was out of the room, Guy returned to see if there was anything else he could remove. The ornate clock on the mantelpiece was silent, frozen at 12:15, the same time he'd discovered it at the day before.

Must be something there to catch it. I hope it can be fixed. I'd like to bring Mum a souvenir, and she could use a nice clock like this.

He opened its front and prodded the second hand. It didn't move. Guy tried rewinding it and was rewarded by a steady *tk-tk-tk*. He decided to give it another chance and left it on the mantel.

Next, he went to tackle the upstairs rooms, starting in the master bedroom. The space made him uneasy after the nightmare, but it needed to be dealt with, and putting it off wouldn't achieve anything. The very first thing he threw out was the baby monitor. A small bubble of satisfaction rose in his chest as the blue plastic thudded into the base of the garbage bag. *Good riddance.*

The dream still lingered in his mind, and when Guy dragged the quilt off the bed, he half expected to find traces of blood underneath. However, the bed sheets were an undisturbed off-white. He released a held breath then stripped the mattress and bundled the sheets into the bag. They were enough to fill it, so he tied it off and went to the window.

The frame was frozen in place. Guy applied his weight to it and was rewarded as the swollen wood shifted. After a moment of straining, the window opened in a rush. Guy grinned as he stuffed the bag through the opening and watched it drop to the ground. The window shortcut would save a lot of time and effort.

Sadly, the mattress was too big to fit through the window. Guy had to carry it down the hallway and stairs, knocking the eerie family portraits askew as he passed them. The fabric smelled horrific enough to make his eyes water. He put it on the back of the pickup truck and used bungee cords to keep it in place.

Lastly, he began emptying the master bedroom's drawers and closet. The drawers were easy—they didn't hold much, mostly just undergarments, hairbrushes, and gloves—but a sense of surrealism washed over Guy as he opened the closet.

A row of dresses confronted him. Guy brushed a finger over the fabric of the first one, a tidy forest-green affair, but he couldn't bring himself to pull it off the rusty hanger.

The clothes humanized the family in a way Guy hadn't felt

before. Even when he was examining the pictures in the stairwell, it was difficult to imagine them as real people with plans, worries, and dreams. But the clothes made them seem almost *too* real. A series of tiny stitches on the sleeve marked where the fabric had torn and been mended. A smudge of powder marred the collar. The style and weight of the fabric made Guy think the mother had sewn it herself in her workroom. *How many hours of effort did she put in to get it just right?*

Don't get sentimental. Guy pulled the dress off the hanger, but he folded it before putting it in the bag. He reached for the dress behind it, but his fingers fell still before touching the fabric.

The sky-blue gown had a sweetheart neckline, and the outline dredged up a memory Guy had almost forgotten: Savannah, in the park, laughing as she tried to coax a duck onto their picnic blanket with the crust from her sandwich. Sunlight danced over her fine, long hair and pale skin. She never wore much makeup, but she loved dresses, and the red outfit with its sweetheart neckline made her look like something out of a dream. Guy remembered joining in her infectious laugh as the duck finally plucked the bread out of her fingers, and thinking he would be a lucky man if he could spend the rest of his life with her.

A keening moan bled out of Guy. He bent forward, fists gripping the dress's fabric and his forehead resting against the sleeve as he fought for control over his emotions. That afternoon with Savannah had once been a happy memory but had become twisted until it held nothing but cutting pain.

"C'mon. *C'mon.* Stop it, you idiot." Guy kicked the corner

of the closet, but he didn't put much effort into the motion. He leaned back, sucking in ragged gasps, and pulled the dress off its hanger. He forced his fingers to release their grip on the fabric and drop it on top of the open bag at his feet, then he reached for the next outfit.

It was a light summery dress. A dark-brown stain smeared the torso. Guy frowned and blinked watering eyes as he pulled the dress out. He held it up to the light to examine the mark.

It almost looks like…

Images of the blood-soaked bed resurfaced, and Guy's stomach clenched. He faced away from the dress, but his mind could still picture the stain, so much like dried blood, blooming across the dress's chest and stomach sections.

It's not blood. It can't be. Why on earth would anyone keep a bloodied dress? She probably spilt wine or some kind of sauce over it and hung it up until she had time to clean it.

The fabric around the stain was stiff and made a disquieting crunching noise as Guy folded it into the bag. He knew it was so old that no stench could remain, but he still breathed through his mouth and held the bag at arm's length as he reached into the closet for the next dress.

It also had a stain across its front. The spot was smaller and more scuffed than the first dress's, but it covered the same areas. Dark drips ran down the skirt.

Guy stared at it. One dress was easy to explain. Two was just strange.

The idea that the family might have been part of some

fundamental religious organization resurfaced. *Maybe one of the cults that sacrificed small animals.*

Guy stuffed the dress into the bag. His uneasiness morphed into discomfort as he drew out a blouse. Only a dozen drop-sized marks dotted the shirt, but they matched the dark liquid on the others and were scattered over the same area.

What the hell happened with this family?

He tried not to see any of the other clothes as he tore them out of the closet, but he caught glimpses of the blood on most articles—and not just the wife's, but also the husband's. It took three bags to clear them all out. Guy didn't breathe easily until the last one was thrown out of the window.

The bedframe was too badly stained by the mattress for anyone to want it, so he spent the following hour disassembling it and throwing it out the window a plank at a time. Cleansing the room was cathartic, and by the time he'd cleared out the last of the unwanted furniture and swept the space, it was unrecognizable.

Hunger gnawed at him, so he set out to make lunch. He put extra effort into it, warming up a can of beans, taking the time to boil water for coffee, and badly burning a slice of bread over the portable stove, then he carried his meal outside, where he could relax in the clear air.

As he scraped the worst of the charring off the toast, he scanned the backyard and the woods surrounding him. The long, weedy grass shifted like an ocean as the wind tugged through it. Farther away, hints of movement drew his attention to the spaces between the trees. He wondered what types of animals lived in the area.

A dark, blocky shape protruded from one of the trees a few yards into the forest. Guy spent a moment squinting at it before he figured out what it was: a tree house. He put his half-eaten beans in the back of the truck and strode toward the trees.

Guy's father had built him a tree house. Holding blocks of wood while his father sawed them were some of Guy's earliest recollections—and part of a cherished collection of memories of his father. The man had passed away from undiagnosed cancer when Guy was four, but the tree house had remained, almost like a tangible part of his father and a space for him to decorate and spend hours inside.

The structure hadn't been as solid as Guy's father had intended. A storm swept through the area a few weeks before Guy's sixth birthday and collapsed the house. In some ways, it felt like losing his father for a second time. Guy's mother had bought him the swing set in an effort to console him. Guy had never told her, but he sometimes still dreamed about the tree house.

Dew clung to Guy's jeans as he waded through the weeds to reach the forest. The tree the tree house had been built on was dying, and part of the trunk had split—possibly from the weight of the house. The blackened branches drooped until the house teetered at an angle, only six feet above the forest floor. It was a little larger than Guy's childhood tree house but still smaller than his bedroom. The floor space would have comfortably held four or five children.

Guy stepped over the remnants of a rotten ladder and strained to see inside the house. Fabric had been tied to the walls, but

Guy's angle was too low to see in properly. Wishing he'd thought to bring his gloves, Guy braced his palms on the doorway, tested his body weight, then pulled himself up.

CHAPTER 11

THE TREE GROANED UNDER the additional pressure and sagged a few inches lower, but the trunk still refused to fully break. Guy carefully lifted himself until he could hang his arms inside the tree house's opening and rest his weight on the cracked wood.

The tree house had been the boy's domain, Guy guessed, based on the blue and red colors and the whittled spear in the corner. Wooden crates and cracked plates had tumbled against the wall when the house had tilted at an angle, but drawings were still stuck to the walls.

Guy squinted as he tried to figure out what the crude pencil art depicted. The same image repeated again and again—a small person wielding a sword against a taller figure with pointed, snarling teeth and outstretched arms.

Is it supposed to be a monster? It was unmistakably human—and female. Guy didn't know if he was reading too much into a child's scribbles, but the woman had been drawn with dark hair—a shade that matched the pictures in the house. *Was he afraid of his mother?*

The stains on the dresses, the disquieting photographs, the remoteness, abandoning their house—the more clues Guy found about Rookward's previous family, the uneasier he felt.

Close to a dozen drawings had been taped around the tree house, each bearing a variation of the dark-haired woman. Sometimes the sword-wielding figure battled her alone; sometimes he stood beside a smaller figure, probably his sister. Guy skimmed the images, then his attention returned to the spear in the corner. It had been fashioned out of a branch with its end whittled into a point. A collection of small rocks had been tucked into a bag beside it, next to what looked like a slingshot.

Was he playing soldier…or preparing to defend himself against an enemy?

Guy's arms were aching from the effort of holding his body weight, so he reluctantly slid back out of the tree house's door and let the structure rebound to its normal position, once again hiding the child's treasure.

Is he still alive? He'd have to be in his late fifties by now. I wonder if there's any way to trace him, or his sister, and find out what really happened here?

Guy didn't like the idea of dismantling the tree house. It would bring back too many memories of losing his own. It was far enough from the yard that its presence probably wouldn't bother the new occupants, so Guy decided it could stay standing for a while longer.

He turned back to Rookward. The dark windows watched him like cold eyes. He shuddered and wrapped his arms around himself.

There's got to be some clue hidden in the house. Almost against his better judgment, Guy had let his curiosity grab hold, and he couldn't shake it. *Something to tell me why they left. Something to explain where they went. What sort of family they were. What happened to the children. Rookward must have the answers—I just need to recognize them when I find them.*

He collected the last of his lunch from the porch and threw it out before returning to the task of cleaning out the rooms. This time, he paid more attention to what he was throwing out. After decluttering old detergent bottles and sponges from the laundry, he uncovered a desk with drawers full of papers in one of the downstairs rooms. He pulled up a seat and spent two hours sifting through the sheets.

From what he could tell, the family's father had worked as a financial advisor for a bank. A lot of the papers talked about investments, interest rates, and appointments. The same name cropped up repeatedly: Thomas Caudwell.

That's weird. It's the same name I dreamed I heard last night.

Guy tried not to let it unsettle him. Thomas was a common name. Besides, he argued, he might have seen the name in the house's deeds or somewhere in the house. His subconscious might have remembered it even though his brain hadn't.

The discovery gave him a new avenue to explore, though. If he could find out the children's names, it might be possible to look them up online or in a phone book.

The papers also gave him the name of the bank Thomas worked at: Westmeyer & Rogers. Guy hadn't heard of it before, but he made a mental note to research it when he went home the next day.

Guy went through the papers carefully, but he didn't find any other details that could help. The most recent date he could find was in April 1965, which was a rejected application for an extended break from work. He packed the papers into a crate to throw out.

Once the study was clear, he reluctantly turned toward the family room.

It was the one part of the house that most needed his attention, and the one he'd been dreading. He donned a mask to protect against the mold and swapped his cloth gloves for heavy-duty plastic ones, then he pushed his way into the room.

For a moment, he stood in the doorway, surveying the wall of vines, the buckled floorboards, and the splotches of black growing across the walls. Then he squared his shoulders and started by clearing the window.

Sheltered inside the house, the vines hadn't been washed by rainfall. Decades of decayed plant matter had built up behind the living vines, and Guy grimaced as he shoveled handfuls of the crusty, slimy substance into a bag.

He took more care around the window frame, where shards of glass poked out between the vegetation and threatened festering, infected cuts. It took nearly half an hour to wiggle all of the shards out of the casing and double-bag them, but once the window was completely empty, Guy was able to throw the bagged trash through it to deal with later.

Next, he went to dismantle the lounge chair. He picked up one of the cushions then stopped. Dark stains spread over its corner and made the fabric crusty and stiff.

Just like the clothes...

Guy prodded the stain, then, against his better judgment, he tugged the mask down to sniff it. The scent of organic, musty decay assaulted him, but the stain didn't hold any odor. Guy supposed it wouldn't, after fifty years.

He felt as though he'd found something important, but he couldn't place it in the jigsaw puzzle in his mind. He moved to throw the cushion through the window then stopped again. *If this is significant, I shouldn't be throwing it out. Especially without documenting it. And I didn't bring a camera, and my phone's battery is dead...*

He faced the chair. More stains dotted the other pillows. Indecision pulled at him for a second, then Guy chose to replace the cushion on the couch. *Just in case. I can always clean it out later if it turns out that it's not important.*

Guy also left the blocky TV in the room's corner; it was too heavy to carry, but once he had new flooring in, he could put it on wheels and roll it out of the room. He bagged the jacket hung on the back of the door. Scraping up the decayed rodent corpses made Guy's skin crawl, but once they were gone, he turned his focus to the floorboards and walls. He only needed to worm up a couple of boards to see the mold hadn't reached the structure, which was a big relief. It would need washing down with bleach, but it wouldn't require rebuilding.

Tearing up the buckled floorboards took longer than he'd planned, though. By the time night set in, he still had half of the floor to finish. With the last of the light, Guy measured the space he would need to reboard and roughed up some calculations for how much wood he would need to purchase. Then it was another rushed bath outside, and he changed into some warmer clothes for night and put the day's clothes into a bag for a deep clean when he got home.

As he sat at the dining room table and chewed on cured meat and canned vegetables by the glow of his gas lamp, Guy ran through a mental list of what still needed to be finished. He'd made good progress on the family room, the only part of the building that needed serious work. He still needed to tear up the carpet in the upstairs rooms and sand the floor down, deal with the wallpaper, repaint, and clear out the remaining clutter. Plus, the yard needed clearing—he would have to see if he could borrow a lawn mower from someone—

A scratching sound pulled Guy's attention up. It reminded him of nails on wood. *An animal in the attic? I keep forgetting about the loose ceiling tiles. There could be more mold up there, too. Lovely.*

He scowled as he continued to eat. Chasing an animal out of the house could throw up a whole host of problems if it was large and inclined to bite. Especially as it was in the highest level of the house, he would just have to hope it was something relatively benign.

The scrabbling was unrelenting, and Guy's subconscious tracked the noise as it traveled from one end of the house and back, the scuffing sound occasionally stopping just above him. He wanted it out, but it was too dark to hunt down the creature that night. Having to keep a flashlight trained on a panicked animal would only handicap him. He would stand a better chance in the morning, with natural light.

Guy spent the remainder of his evening cutting up and bagging the guest room's carpet. The work was tedious with only the gas lamp to light it, and he gave up shortly after nine. The scrabbling continued intermittently, keying his nerves tightly, but he was exhausted enough to think it wouldn't keep him awake. He was right. Once he got into his sleeping bag, he only remembered rolling over once before sleep dragged him under.

CHAPTER 12

April 1965

"THEN WE'LL MOVE!" LOUISE slapped her tea towel onto the counter and began untying her apron. "We'll move, *again*, and you can get a job somewhere else, as long as they don't examine your references too closely—"

"Stop it." Thomas let the plate slide back into the sink. Louise's frantic struggle with her apron's knot only made it tighter. He came up behind her and took over, gradually easing the ties out. She sighed and slumped forward while he worked.

"I'm sorry. I'm just—"

"I know. Me, too."

"It's exhausting." Her voice was ragged. She wiped at her face, and Thomas knew she wanted him to think the dampness came from the sink's steam, so he didn't say anything. She swallowed.

"The constant worry. You're getting almost no sleep. Something's got to give."

"I know."

"And our savings are almost gone…" She lifted her head and waved a hand at the room. "This beautiful house. You thought it would let you get away from her, didn't you?"

Thomas didn't answer. He'd initially couched the idea of moving into the forest as a metaphorical sea change. *The children will have more room to play! Safer than the city! We could afford a bigger house!* He'd never told Louise the real driving force had been Amy. She must have just guessed. She knew him too well for him to hide much.

The knot came undone, and Louise pulled off the apron. Her face was drawn and gray, and she wouldn't meet his eyes. "It's true, isn't it? We moved all the way out here to get away from her, and she followed us anyway."

Thomas licked his lips. "Maybe you're right. Maybe we should move again. Go somewhere far away. Change our names. Maybe it's the only way to get free of this."

"The kids…" Louise groaned and rested her back against the kitchen counter. "They'll hate it. They've only just gotten used to here."

"They'll adjust."

"Can we even afford it? We were stretching our finances to buy this place, and if you have to give up your job, as well—"

"Mum."

Both Thomas and Louise startled. Daniel stood in the open

kitchen door, his face pinched and unhappy. Rebecca hovered just behind him, holding her toy bear so tightly that she looked as though she were strangling it.

"What's wrong?" Thomas glanced toward the window. The yard was empty. He hated himself for being so on edge all the time.

Daniel scuffed his shoe on the mat. "That lady was here again. You wanted me to tell you if I saw her."

"Where?" Thomas pressed closer to the window. It had been his job to watch the children while they played outside, but the argument had drawn his attention away. "Did she come out of the forest?"

"Yep," Rebecca piped up. Her voice held the petulant tilt that seemed perfectly judged to fray Thomas's nerves, but he felt too sick to be bothered by it. "She said mean stuff. She said Mummy was a horse."

"Whore," Daniel corrected.

Louise made a faint choking noise then swept forward and scooped Rebecca into her arms. She grabbed Daniel's hand and began tugging him into the dining room.

Thomas knew he wasn't responsible, but guilt made his palms sweaty. "Lou. Where are you going?"

"To find Georgie." Her eyes were round and wild, and her cheeks were sheet-white. "*You* can start thinking about how we'll get a new house."

Thomas braced his hands on the counter and listened to Louise murmuring to the children. He kept scanning the tree line, his focus skimming back and forth over the space, as he waited for his nausea to subside.

She was right there. Out in the open. Talking to my children. I was supposed to be watching them. And I didn't see—

He snatched a plate out of the sink and hurled it against the wall. Its shattered fragments tumbled to the floor as Thomas pressed his palms against his closed eyes. He felt colder than the temperature allowed for.

She slinks closer every day. She won't be satisfied until she's destroyed our lives. We can move, but what if she follows again? Even if we change our names, even if we go into hiding, she'll never stop searching for us. Never.

He stared into the forest. She was in there, somewhere, perhaps watching him even as he helplessly searched for her. Thomas felt stretched unbearably thin; he didn't know how much longer he could hold on before he snapped.

His gaze fell to the chopping block beside the sink. The knife handles glittered in the dull light.

"I'm going outside," Thomas called.

It only took a second for Louise to appear in the doorway, Georgie cradled in her arms, her face tense. "Why?"

"I don't know. To see if I can break the stalemate." He pulled the longest knife out of the block. He'd only ever used it to cut vegetables, and holding it in a defensive stance felt strange. "To see if I can get us free, somehow."

"She's dange—"

"I know." He ducked forward to press a kiss to Louise's

cheek. She didn't return it, but the tightness around her eyes loosened.

"Thomas, be safe." She followed him to the kitchen door.

It was still unlocked from the children's play session, so he pushed the wooden slab open then handed her the key. She squeezed his hand when their fingers came into contact, then Thomas stepped outside and shivered against the wind. The day was colder than it had appeared.

He waited for Louise to lock the door behind him, then he began moving toward the forest. When he looked over his shoulder, he could make out Louise's pale face in the kitchen window and glimpses of the top of Georgie's head as she bounced him in her arms.

Thomas flexed sweating fingers around the knife's handle. His lungs ached every time he drew air into them. The wind snatched at his shirt and hair and wormed through every tiny hole in the fabric. It felt like icy fingers brushing over his skin, and Thomas repressed a shudder.

Her eyes followed him—he was sure of it—but he couldn't see her. He stopped at the clearing's edge and squinted into the kaleidoscope of shadows between the trees. He set his shoulders and put conviction into his voice. "I want to talk!"

A branch snapped somewhere to his right. Thomas swiveled in its direction, but he couldn't tell if the cause had been man-made or natural. His mouth was dry. He swirled his tongue over his teeth in an effort to wet them. "I know you're there. Come out and talk to me."

A small animal chattered as it darted through the branches. Dead leaves fluttered past Thomas's shoulders. He thought he saw motion a few dozen paces ahead of himself, buried among the trees and vines, and moved toward it.

The knife felt heavy. He tried to keep his grip on it tight, but doubts were screaming through his mind. *Can I really go through with this? Even if she's pure evil, even after the hell she's put my family through, can I murder her in cold blood?*

Yes, he answered himself. *Because if you don't, she'll keep moving closer, and closer, until she's breathing over you as you sleep.* He straightened his back and tightened his grip on the knife, but that couldn't stop his hand from trembling visibly. *Your family needs this.*

The wind formed a strange echo as it wormed its way through the boughs. The rustles, creaks, and scrapes of moving branches enveloped Thomas. They masked any sounds a human might make and disoriented him as he hunted for more signs of motion among the rough-textured trunks and vines snaking across his field of vision.

It hadn't been so bad when he was in the clearing, out in the open, where he could watch his back. But inside the woods, he could be within an arm's length of Amy and wouldn't even know she was there until her nails raked over his skin.

He fought the shiver that wanted to run through him. Signs of weakness would only make things worse. He had to keep his voice hard and commanding and his actions purposeful, no matter how badly he wanted to retreat to the clearing.

"Stay away from my family." He raised his voice to make sure she heard, even though it cracked. "Come near them again, and I'll…I'll kill you."

The words sounded phony. He couldn't stop the tremor in the hand holding the knife, and he knew the glint of shaking metal would be easy to see in the dim forest.

Thomas hadn't used his hands for violence since schoolyard scraps when he was a child. He tried to visualize slicing the blade into Amy, sinking it into the space between her ribs and watching bright-red blood pour over his fingers. The image filled him with sick horror.

I can't do it. The image morphed. Thomas pictured Amy in front of him, her arms held wide and a manic smile stretching her pale lips. His arms were like rubber; she nudged the blade aside as though it were cardboard then stepped closer, the pale fingers reaching forward to envelop him…

I can't. He was about to be sick. *I can't kill her, and I can't win.*

An animal scurried across dried leaves, and Thomas flinched. He began backing toward the forest's edge, trying to watch all sides without seeming flighty. Amy loved weakness, fed on it, delighted in it. It would be dangerous to give her that pleasure.

Something glittered on the tree to his right. The bark had been cut, and amber sap beaded around the scores. The damage had been on the wrong side of the trunk to see when walking forward but was clearly visible in retreat. Thomas's nerves were wound to their breaking point, and his mind screamed for him to get back to the sanctuary of his house's threshold, but a dark curiosity held him still. The marks created a word, and he knew what it would say before he even read it.

Thomas.

He touched the cuts. Golden sap dribbled from them and ran down the rough bark, but it was long dry. He stepped back and saw his name on another tree, and then another, and another. Nausea rose, and the metallic taste of panic flooded his mouth.

Has she marked every tree in the damn forest?

A branch cracked behind him. Thomas's fractured courage broke. He ran.

His breath was ragged, and his pulse throbbed as he burst out of the woods. She was just behind him, he knew, her arm outstretched to snag his shirt, and he reflexively arched his back to avoid the stab of her fingernails.

He hit the kitchen door. The thud jarred him, and he blinked watering eyes as he turned to the clearing. It was bare. He lifted his gaze toward the woods, but they appeared just as barren as always.

She was still watching him, though. Her attention was unrelenting, heavier than a cinder block tied around his neck. A soft click sounded as Louise unlocked the door, then the solid wood disappeared from his back.

"What happened?" Louise's voice was hoarse. She took his arm, her fingers shaky as she pulled him into the house.

Thomas couldn't bring himself to look at her. Sweat beaded over his skin, running down the gap between his shoulder blades, as he backed into the kitchen. He didn't move his attention from the woods.

"I don't know. I didn't see her, but she was there. Somehow. She won't show herself, but she's there, watching us, watching our children…and I don't know what to do anymore."

"What happened to the knife?"

He glanced down. He didn't remember releasing the blade, but his hands were empty. Dread filled his chest like a cold weight as he lifted his eyes to the shifting trees.

She has it now.

CHAPTER 13

THE SOUND OF BREAKING glass was so loud and real that it came through Guy's sleep. He sat up, blinking slowly in the dim light, and stared about the room in a fugue of tiredness.

Just another dream. That's all.

The images were foggy and fading quickly. The dream had been about words floating in a forest, he thought. And two children. Something bad had happened, and he was worried for the kids. For half a second, he managed to recall their faces—round and pouting, a hard glare for the boy and a halo of curls for the girl—then the image dissolved.

Guy lay back down and adjusted the pillow. The chilled air drew goose bumps over his arms, but that night, he'd been prepared and covered the sleeping bag with extra blankets. He closed his eyes and waited to drift back under.

Whispers scratched at his ears. Guy snapped his eyes open

but kept still, breath held, to listen. He was sure he'd heard a woman's voice coming from deeper in the house. The world seemed to hang in suspension for a moment, then a floorboard on the ground floor groaned.

Ignore it. Your imagination is going wild again. Guy squeezed his hands into fists and took deliberately slow breaths. *You've been through this house too often to imagine you're not alone. Just go back to sleep.*

The dead tree's branches scrabbled against the stones somewhere below Guy's window. A night animal shrieked. The swing's ropes groaned with aching perseverance. Guy forced his eyes closed and narrowed his attention to the air moving through his lungs.

"Softly—quietly—"

He sat up. The words had been faint, as though echoed through a tunnel, but they were unmistakable. His throat tightened.

A door shifted open. The sound stretched out far longer than it should have, fraying Guy's nerves and spiking his heart rate.

His mind warred for a moment. He'd already wasted one night chasing his imagination through the building, and he didn't want a repeat. On the other hand… *What if this time is genuine?*

The branches continued to scrabble. A gust of wind knocked something over—perhaps one of the tools he'd left in the family room—and it hit the floor with a bang. Guy tried to swallow, but his mouth felt like a desert.

The tension was viciously unrelenting, threatening to make his heart explode. Against his better judgment, he crawled out of his bed and blindly searched for the crowbar he'd left on the table. He hadn't thought to bring the flashlight up with him that night, but he didn't want to waste time lighting the gas lamp. Instead, he clenched his fist around the metal, crept to the door, twisted the handle as softly as he could, and peered down the hallway.

Moonlight came through the doors he'd left open. It painted bands of washed-out blue light across the hallway runner and wallpaper, playing tricks with Guy's vision. He hesitated in the doorway a moment and strained his ears.

Whispers floated through the house. Guy struggled to latch on to the words, but it was like listening to static. The only thing he could tell was that they came from the lower floor. He flexed his grip on the crowbar and started along the hallway, staying close to the wall and rolling his bare feet to minimize the noise.

A windowpane rattled, making Guy flinch. He peered into the room—the girl's bedroom—and felt an ache start deep in his chest as he watched the curtains roll in the wind. They looked too much like a living figure dancing in the wind.

The whispers had fallen quiet, but his ears still strained to hear them among the house's natural noises. He followed the hallway's bend. Moonlight glinted off the top of the staircase's railing. Guy fixed his eyes on it as he slipped forward, his inhalations shallow and body hunched.

A strange, unnerving tingle crawled along his spine. He felt as though he were being followed—and closely. The presence lurked barely a pace behind him, so close that he should be able to feel its breath on his bare skin, its fingers hovering just above his shoulder. A drop of perspiration rolled down the back of his neck. He couldn't draw air. He wanted to turn—to confront the sudden terror that had gripped him—but the insane part of his mind screamed for him to keep his focus ahead. As long as he didn't look, it might not be real. As long as he didn't turn around, he wouldn't have to confront it.

Stop it. Stop it! The crowbar shook, even though he squeezed it with both hands. *You're scaring yourself for no reason. There's nothing here! Rookward House is empty!*

A door on the ground floor slammed. Guy leaped and bit down on a yelp. He teetered at the top of the stairs and, for a second, thought he might fall. Then he stumbled back and pressed his shoulder blades to the wall.

The whispers returned. They rattled on the lower floor, seeming to bounce at him from every direction, their tone urgent and demanding. Guy didn't give fear a second chance to freeze him. He darted down the stairs, keeping his footfalls as light as he could while his heart beat a tattoo against his ribs. He skidded to a halt in the foyer. A floorboard shifted inside the guest room. Guy advanced toward it, crowbar held ahead of himself, and used a foot to nudge the door open.

The space's dimensions seemed wrong with half of its carpet torn up. The moonlight helped create a surreal pall over the area, distorting colors and stretching shadows. The wood-and-bronze mantelpiece clock had frozen again: 12:15.

Behind Guy, someone inhaled. Fear burst through his nerves

like electricity as he swiveled. A woman stood in the doorway, moonlight flashing across her wild eyes as long hair flowed around her face. She opened bloodless lips, and a shriek deafened him.

Guy screamed, as well. He swung the crowbar. His aim was poor; it missed the woman and thwacked into the wooden doorframe. Her shriek rose in pitch, then she staggered back from him, arms raised over her head, as she cried, "Don't hurt me! *Don't* hurt me!"

Guy lurched back as a gangly figure appeared beside the girl. Something clicked, then an explosion of light engulfed him. He blinked against the flashlight's beam as the figures, which had appeared inhuman in the moonlight, resolved into teenagers.

"What the hell, man!" The boy was tall and thin, and too-long hair hung around his twisted face.

"What the hell yourself!" Guy brandished the crowbar at them, but he didn't put much force into the gesture. They weren't the terror-effusing phantoms his mind had conjured; they were only kids, who were clearly afraid of him. "What are you doing in my house?"

"I thought it was empty!" The girl's face was sheet-white. She straightened her back and gripped the lapels of her jacket. "It-it's always been empty! Since forever!"

Guy blew out air through his nose and let his shoulders slump. He waved toward the boy. "Get that light out of my eyes. You scared me."

"*You* scared *us*, man." The beam shifted to point at the ground.

Its refracted light put strange shadows over their faces. "And you nearly brained my girlfriend."

"It was my fault." She spoke quickly and pulled at her partner's sleeve. "I came up behind him by accident. Come on, let's go. Sorry, Mister, we didn't mean to disturb you. We wouldn't have come if we'd known someone was staying here."

Guy put the crowbar on the fireplace's mantelpiece. He'd been holding it so tightly that his fingers ached when he flexed them, so he ran them through his hair to give them something to do. Clarity was starting to filter through his sleep-dazed, fear-fogged mind. "It's fine. Hang on, you don't have to run off straightaway. How'd you get here?"

The boy glared at his friend. She squared her shoulders and answered. "We drove, of course. Didn't you hear our car?"

"I was asleep. It must be well past midnight."

"Nearly three in the morning, yeah."

Guy narrowed his eyes at the pair. They were bundled in warm jackets and thick pants, but other than that, they made an odd couple. The boy was sallow and surly, but his friend seemed to smile easily, even though the expression was more nervous than happy. She was short but held a bouncy kind of energy that made her seem bigger than she was. In the dim light, it was possible to mistake her long, fine hair for Savannah's. The idea tightened Guy's throat, and he tried not to focus on it. "Okay, it's even later than I thought. That leads to my other question. What are you two doing here at three in the morning?"

The girl answered, her tone a little defensive. "We were

curious. About the legends. I wanted to see if there was anything left of Amy."

Amy. The name was familiar, and it felt significant, but Guy struggled to place it. He raised a hand to stop the teens from backing down the hallway. They were technically trespassing, but now that his heart was slowing and the adrenaline was subsiding, he realized he didn't want them to leave. If they did, he would be alone again, just him and the house, sitting in darkness until morning. He suppressed a shudder. "Hold up a moment. I want to hear about that. Why don't you stay a bit? I'll make some coffee."

They looked at each other. The girl's eyes shone with excitement, but her partner's face twisted.

Guy chuckled. "It's fine. I can promise you I'm not crazy. I inherited this place. I'm doing some repairs before putting it on the market. You said something about legends?"

"We can stay," the girl said, poking her partner's arm. "Right?"

He shrugged and scowled. "Whatever."

"Guy." He extended a hand.

The girl shook it, her grin stretching her cheeks. "I'm Tiff. And this is Blake. I'd love something warm to drink."

CHAPTER 14

THE GAS LAMP CREATED a bubble of light in the dining room. Guy had only brought one mug for himself, so he hunted through his supplies for substitutes as the pot of water boiled over the gas stove.

"I should have known someone was here." Tiff sat at the table, arms folded in front of herself, as she watched Guy. "The gate was missing. I just figured the government had finally taken it away or something."

Guy found a glass measuring jug and a small saucepan. They weren't classic cup material, but he figured they'd do in a pinch. He infused some laughter into his words so that Tiff would know he wasn't irritable. "And the building supplies everywhere didn't give it away?"

She shrugged, appearing wholly unashamed. "I wanted to explore the place with the lights off. We really couldn't see much."

"Uh-huh." Guy blinked at Blake, who leaned far back in his chair with his arms crossed. He didn't seem happy. Guy was struck by the impression that the expedition hadn't been his idea, and he'd only gone along with it because he was hoping to get lucky. Guy's presence had tanked that possibility, and he was sulking. "So, tell me again why you're exploring Rookward? Some sort of bravery test?"

"I guess you could call it that." Tiff picked at a splinter poking out of the tabletop. "You know this place's history, right?"

"'Fraid not. My mother inherited it, but she forgets things easily." *Like forgetting she owned a house in the first place.* The pot boiled, so Guy spooned instant coffee into the containers and doled out the water. He passed the mug to Tiff, gave her boyfriend the measuring jug, and kept the saucepan for himself. "You said a name. Amy. Who is she?"

"Pure evil, if you believe the legends." Tiff grinned and wrapped her hands around her mug.

She seemed to have a flair for the dramatic, and Guy thought she was enjoying the attention. That suited Guy—he had no chance of sleeping again that night, and a good story would help pass the time until dawn. He leaned back in his chair and nodded for her to continue.

"The story's pretty well-known in our area, but I guess it didn't spread far. So basically, there was this family living here, right? Parents and their three kids. And this woman, Amy, knew the father from work. She fell in love with him and must have been at least a bit crazy, because she started stalking him and was

101

obsessed with being his wife. She lived in the forest like a wild animal, watching the house and sometimes digging up the garden or leaving messages. The family called the police, but the police couldn't find her even though they scoured the woods multiple times, and eventually gave up. So the father—"

"Thomas," Guy interjected.

"Right, Thomas, he didn't want to leave his family alone with Amy, so he stopped going to work. They holed up in their house and kept the doors locked at all times. They figured Amy would eventually have to give up; she'd starve or freeze at night or something. But she didn't. It went on for weeks, gradually escalating, until the family decided they had to move." Tiff sipped her drink and crinkled her nose. "This is gross."

"Sorry. I'm roughing it. There's, uh, water, or…" He narrowed his eyes at them. "Are either of you old enough to drink?"

They exchanged a glance. "Sure."

"Of course."

Liars. Guy shook his head as he tried to hide a grin then rose to dig through his boxes. *I wasn't much different when I was their age.*

Tucked next to a bag of rice was a bottle of brandy he'd been saving for either a celebration or a pity party, depending on how his time at the house went. He opened it, poured a measure into his saucepan, then pushed the bottle across the table. "Help yourselves."

Blake, his glare challenging Guy to call him out, took a swig straight out of the bottle. He passed it to Tiff, who sniffed it, then dribbled less than a teaspoon into her mug. She swirled the mix experimentally.

"So…" Guy tapped his fingers on the tabletop. "The family left. Do you know where they went?"

Tiff looked up. "Oh, no, they didn't leave. That's the whole point of the story. Amy must have heard about their plans somehow. She broke into the house and murdered them."

Guy's inhale caught in his throat. He had to cough to clear it. "Murdered? All of them?"

"Mm-hm." She sniffed her mug but didn't drink from it. "That's why Rookward is infamous. Amy went through the building and stabbed the family one by one. And do you want to know the worst bit? They weren't discovered for, like, four days. The house was so far from town, y'know, no one made deliveries to it or anything. People didn't think anything was wrong until the mother didn't return her friends' phone calls for a couple of days."

Guy ran a hand over his mouth. He felt as though the ground had fallen out from under him. The idea that the family was dead had occurred to him—but in a distant way. He'd imagined them involved in a car accident or passing away in hospital from an epidemic. Not *murdered.*

An image rose in his mind: the clothes in the upstairs closet saturated with dark stains. Guy frowned. He didn't remember the fabric being cut.

Tiff's eyes glittered, and the corners of her mouth twitched up. "It took four days for the police to show up. Amy stayed in the house the entire time. They say she dressed the family up in different outfits and dragged their bodies through the rooms for dinner, bedtime, playtime—all while they were decaying."

The wooden dining table under Guy's hands suddenly felt repulsive. He pictured the family of corpses arranged around it, plates and cutlery set out for them, their dead, bulging eyes unfocused and heads lolled against their shoulders. "You're making this up. You've got to be."

"She's not." Blake snorted and reached for the brandy bottle again. "Everyone knows the story. Some people even kept newspaper clippings from when it all went down. They found bloodstains in the chairs, in the beds, even in the car. She took them out for a drive. She was crazy, man."

When Blake set the bottle back onto the table, Guy snatched it up and poured more brandy into his coffee. Then he lifted the saucepan and took a gulp. The alcohol burned as it went down, but he knew it would dull some of the ache in his chest. "That's messed up. Did she go to jail?"

"Nope." Tiff propped her chin up on her folded hands, elbows balanced on the table. "Apparently, she'd been expecting the police. She was in the TV room, freshly dead. She'd heard the cars coming, sat on the couch next to her beloved, and cut her own throat. They say, when the police found her, she was smiling."

Blake reached out for the bottle. Guy handed it back then scratched his fingers through his hair. He felt dirty, not just on the outside where Rookward's grime had been building up, but on the inside, too.

He understood why his grandfather hadn't done anything with the house after inheriting it. Perhaps he'd even tried to sell it but couldn't find any buyers. So he'd just hidden the deeds in a box of receipts in the attic and left it to rot.

Tiff sipped at her coffee and grimaced. "You got any milk for this?"

"Sorry, no fridge." Guy, still in a fugue of thought, shook his head. "Well, I mean, there is a fridge—but there's no power."

"You can't get it turned on?"

"No. The original family had a generator around the back, but it's long dead. I don't think the house ever got hooked up to the grid, so to speak." Guy shrugged and gulped more of his coffee-brandy cocktail. "Just one of the things I've got to figure out before I sell this place."

"I guess you must be related to the family that lived here, huh?" She tilted her head to the side, her long hair shimmering in the golden light. "Sorry if I was being insensitive."

"No, it's fine. If they were relatives, I didn't know them. This was the first I'd heard of…well, any of this." Guy cracked a smile. "I'm not planning to stay here, anyway. The idea was to fix it and sell it. Then my mother and I can move somewhere new and start a fresh life."

"Why're you moving?" Tiff pushed her cup aside and blinked at him. "Why not spend the money on a holiday to Europe or something? That's what I'd do."

Guy swallowed a chuckle. "I don't really fit into my town anymore. I need to go somewhere no one knows me."

"Ooh." She bent forward, and mischief narrowed her eyes. "Those are the words of a social pariah. What'd you do? Must be bad to make people hate you. This girl at my school had an affair with a married teacher, and everyone found out. The bullying was so bad she had to be homeschooled. Did something like that happen to you?"

Guy snorted. "Not that exactly. And I'd rather not talk about it."

"Come on, we told you all about your stupid house!"

"That's in no way a fair trade." Guy chuckled and tilted his head back to stare at the ceiling. The white plaster was discolored. In the gold light of his lamp, it was reminiscent of clouds caught in a sunset. The words were out of him before he knew what he was doing. "I made a horrible mistake and hurt someone I cared about."

"Go on." Tiff's cheeky smile was equal parts infuriating and funny.

Guy shook his head. "You kids live locally, don't you?"

"About forty minutes away."

"Right, so you wouldn't have heard the story. It was all over my local newspaper, though." Guy's smile faded as he rubbed at the faint tan line where his engagement ring had once rested. "I had a fiancée called Savannah. We were in love. For a while, I thought she might actually be my soulmate, if you believe in such a thing. She was perfect—sweet and smart and one of the kindest people you'd ever meet. But…well, I didn't have much money, and my work contract was coming to an end. The bills were growing, and it was stressing me out. I—" It took a lot of effort to say the words. "I've always had a problem with my temper. I get angry easily. Never violent. I don't hit people or anything. I just kind of…blow up and scream a bunch and have to apologize afterward."

Tiff squinted at him. "You don't look like an angry sort of person."

"Thanks, I guess?" He pulled a face. "You don't look like the sort of kid who'd be interested in a place like Rookward."

"Fair enough."

"Well, for what it's worth, I'd been working on my temper. I saw a counselor for a while when I could afford it. And Savannah was really understanding and patient, even though I knew her family didn't like me."

"So what happened?" Tiff, impatient, drummed her fingers on the table.

Blake had zoned out of the conversation and was picking dirt out from under his nails. Guy was tempted to laugh again. *Poor kid just wanted a make-out session. Now he's stuck hearing my life story.*

"I found a half-empty bottle of vitamins in Savannah's purse. 'Specially formulated for the first trimester of pregnancy.'" Guy flexed his shoulders as a shiver of stress—a leftover echo from the memory—crawled over him. "She'd been keeping it a secret. We didn't have much money, and she was scared I'd be angry. Well, she wasn't wrong. I…I yelled at her. I wasn't even angry about the baby. I just felt furious that she hadn't trusted me enough to tell me." Smiling hurt. "Ironic, huh?"

"Did you want her to get rid of it?"

"No. Absolutely not. I wanted to be a father. The…the timing was bad, but we would have made it work. Somehow. But I exploded like the idiot I am, and Savannah stormed off rather than listen to me yell. I realized I needed to get out of the house—that was one of the coping methods the counselor suggested, just remove myself from the situation—so I got in the car to go for a drive." The pain felt like molten lava, blindingly hot and boiling out of his stomach to burn his throat. "I didn't realize she'd come out of the house. I didn't see her behind the car. I was so angry I hadn't checked the mirror—I hit her—"

The thud. The cry. The rush of horror. The lurch as he tried to stop the car from rolling back over her. They'd replayed through Guy's dreams for weeks after it, each time just as raw, awful, and unforgivable as reality. Metallic blood seeped across his tongue where he'd bitten it without realizing. "She lived. The baby, too, by some miracle. They're worried it will be affected, though. Were worried—it would have been born a few weeks ago—I don't know if…"

Tiff bent low over the table, chin resting on her forearms. She'd been mercifully quiet while he told his story in broken fragments, almost as though she'd known he needed to share it. "Is that why you need to leave town? You're scared of bumping into her on the street?"

"Yes. And no." The chuckle hurt, and he crossed his arms over his torso. "Savannah assumed I hit her deliberately. I didn't—I swear I didn't. I loved her even when I was angry at her. But she thought I'd lost control in a big way. Her family had been warning her about me for years, saying it was an abusive relationship and would escalate if she didn't get out, and she finally believed them. Her parents made sure it went to court. Attempted manslaughter. I was acquitted for lack of evidence, but wow. I turned into the town's own OJ Simpson. Legally innocent, but everyone believed I was blatantly guilty."

"OJ eventually got jail time, though," Blake said.

Tiff smacked his shoulder. "Stop it. Insensitive jerk."

"Nah, it's all right." This time, the chuckle felt a little more natural. "It's good to talk about it to someone impartial. Thanks for listening."

Tiff pursed her lips. "It's a sad story. Might even be more miserable than this house's. You're all alone now, right?"

"Mostly." He picked at a scratch running along the table's edge. "My friends sent a few supportive text messages during the court case, but they've avoided talking to me since. My mum believes me, though. Bless her."

"Well, I hope you can sell this house and move away like you want to. Rookward is pretty notorious in the town, but you might be able to snag an out-of-state buyer or something."

"Fingers crossed," Guy agreed. Eager to change the subject, he said, "I'm still a bit foggy on why you're here. Did you just want to mosey around a fifty-year-old crime scene, or…?"

She shrugged. "Pretty much. I drive down the lane twice a week to get to softball practice, and the gate was missing yesterday. It looked like someone had driven down the path. Like

I said, I assumed the government was finally doing something about the property. I thought it might be my last chance to visit before it was torn down or something. So I convinced Blake to come with me. I wanted to see if the house was as creepy as people said, and if it was really haunted."

"Ghost stories, huh?" *I shouldn't be surprised. It's the scene of multiple murders; of course people would be predisposed to imagine specters live here. And a house this old is bound to have some bizarre quirks to reinforce the theory—just look at how many times I've managed to scare myself while staying here, and I don't even believe in ghosts.*

"When I was a kid, my older sister visited with her boyfriend a couple of times. She says she saw Amy's ghost walking through the windows." Tiff held her arms out ahead of herself, hands limp, and mimed a zombie's shuffle. She laughed as she slumped back in her chair. "I'm, like, ninety percent sure she made it up to scare me. But I was curious, y'know?"

"I can believe that." The earliest hints of dawn were starting to spread natural light through the dining room. Guy's focus was drawn to the tiny chips and scratches in the table, the age stains across the ceiling, the grimy window, and the floral china closeted away in the cabinet. "I feel the same way."

CHAPTER 15

"YOU'RE SOBER ENOUGH TO drive?" Guy asked Blake. They paced around the outside of the house, toward the front yard. The teen was just as surly as normal, but half of the brandy bottle had disappeared while they were talking, and Guy knew he hadn't put that much in his coffee.

"Sure." Blake shrugged nonchalantly.

Tiff gave him a shrewd-eyed scan then held out her hand. "I'll drive. It's my car, anyway."

He looked ready to argue, but Tiff lowered her eyebrows, and he sighed as he passed her the keys. "Whatever."

They made a beeline for the old sedan parked near the house's front door.

"I feel like I should thank you for visiting, or something," Guy said. "Even though you broke in. Sorry for almost knocking your head off, Tiff."

"It's cool. Sorry for smashing your window."

"You—what?"

She gave him a sheepish smile. "I didn't realize the back door was open."

Guy remembered being woken by a smashing noise and smothered a groan. Glass was expensive. "That's all right. Drive safely. Stay in school, don't do drugs, drink lots of water. Et cetera."

Tiff laughed as she leaped into the driver's seat. Blake raised a hand in goodbye as he slipped through the passenger's door, then the car's engine rumbled to life.

Guy backed up as he watched the car trundle toward the narrow path through the woods. A low-level headache had come on the tail of the disturbed sleep and elevated stress, but Guy wasn't unhappy about the surprise visit. After spending nearly two days alone with the house, it was nice to talk to another human.

And she looked so much like Savannah.

Guy scuffed his boot on the doorstep. It wasn't completely true; both Tiff and Savannah had pale skin and long, fine hair, but the similarities ended there. Tiff was short, bouncy, and a little flighty. Savannah was tall, graceful, and sweet. Her large eyes and long neck had sometimes reminded him of a gentle deer, almost painfully lovely and far too good for him.

Even after the accident, he didn't think she'd truly hated him. The day in court was branded into his memory. The bruises had faded by that point, but she'd still been wearing the wrist cast and walked with a limp. Her family surrounded her, nudging her forward and shooting Guy hateful glares, and Guy had prepared for the worst as Savannah took the stand.

The judge had been sympathetic toward her. All she would have had to do was embellish the facts a little, and Guy would have been in jail. But she hadn't. He could still picture her, nervous eyes fixed on the table, hands clasped tightly, as she spoke. She'd softened a lot of the details, omitted others, and skirted around the truth. She hadn't wanted Guy to end up in jail, and the case had been dismissed based on her testimony.

It had given Guy a small, urgent hope that the relationship might still be saved. He'd tried to speak to Savannah on the way out of the court, but she wouldn't look at him no matter how loudly he called her name. As he watched her get into the backseat of her parents' car, he'd realized she didn't want him in her life anymore.

And so Guy had tried to respect her wishes. He knew he could probably demand visitation rights for his child, but he didn't feel right putting Savannah in that situation after she'd spared him. The best thing he could do was to leave her alone to rebuild her life.

A spark of frustration bloomed in his chest then fizzled out. He lost his temper less since the accident. Sometimes it still surprised him—like the fury at the upstairs door during his first day at Rookward—but more often, the anger was a painful reminder of what he'd lost. It evoked a wave of sadness that doused the rage before it could take hold.

Guy folded his arms across his chest. He shivered in the cold air and turned his mind to Tiff's story to distract himself from the pain. She'd given him a lot of history about the house, but he wasn't sure he was better for the knowledge.

Be careful how much of it you trust. He stepped through Rookward's kitchen door. *It's a fifty-year-old urban legend. Almost all of it could be fictionalized.*

And yet, he was surrounded by evidence. Guy hesitated in the dining room, staring at the table that had likely once sat a family of corpses, and shuddered. He was due to drive back to his mother's that morning, and he couldn't deny it would be a relief to sit in her smaller kitchen instead of Rookward's. He moved toward the family room.

The crusty stains across the sofa took on a new significance. They'd matched the marks on the clothing in the upstairs bedroom. Guy pictured an insane woman carefully undressing and redressing the corpses, changing their clothes each morning, for four days while she waited for the police to find her. Some of the stains would be blood. Some would be fluids produced by the early stages of decomposition.

Guy felt faintly sick. He retreated from the family room without touching anything.

I was wrong. The family wasn't weird. They were just a normal family trapped in an awful situation.

He remembered the drawings and the homemade spear in the tree house. The boy had been defending his family against a dark-haired, pointy-toothed woman.

I hope they didn't suffer. Guy lingered in the hallway. It was shocking to think of how abruptly the family's existence had been snuffed out. There were plates in the kitchen sink and stains on the chopping board; he wondered if that meant they had been interrupted shortly after dinner.

And was Amy the reason the children all slept in the one room? I wouldn't want my family scattered across the house if I were being stalked—

A fresh twinge of pain pulled at Guy's aching insides as he thought of Savannah and her baby. *His* baby. One of his friends had told him it was a girl, but he didn't even know her name.

Face forward. He'd repeated the mantra to himself a thousand times since the accident. *Regret will drag you down, smother you, kill you. You've got to face forward. Try your hardest. Do what you can to improve the world while you have the chance.*

He gazed about Rookward. It had been the scene of great suffering. But there was no rule saying it couldn't ever experience joy again. Maybe, in a few months, a new family would live in it. Children might grow up there. Their parents might laugh as they repainted the rooms together. Good memories could be superimposed over the painful.

Just got to keep facing forward.

Guy rubbed his fingertips over his eyelids and rolled his shoulders. His muscles were still stiff from the cold, and his fingers were growing numb. He'd fetched his shoes and a jacket from upstairs before making the teens their coffee, but the pajamas he still wore underneath were nowhere near thick enough to shield him against the chill.

He jogged upstairs to change and brush his teeth, spitting the water and toothpaste out of the window, then rubbed his hands together as he returned to the ground floor.

The hallways felt alien in the gray morning light. The shredded wallpaper rustled as his movements created eddies of air in the still, dusty space. The floorboards groaned under his weight, and the mournful strains left an uneasy echo bouncing between the walls.

Guy ran his hands through his hair as he reached the foyer. He'd donned the same clothes from the day before, and they felt dirty enough to make his skin crawl. He was craving home—the idea of a hot shower and warm meal was like a siren song—but it seemed wasteful to leave early in the morning when he could still squeeze in another few hours of work.

The front door caught his eye. It was still boarded shut and overrun by vines. He could save himself a fair bit of trouble on his next visit to the house if he had a second way in and out. And with clean clothes and shampoo just a few hours away, there would be no better time to wade into what promised to be grimy work.

The door was locked on the inside with three bolts, so Guy undid them and tried to open it. The boards nailing it shut creaked but didn't budge. Guy scrunched his mouth up and resigned himself to getting it open the hard way.

He retrieved his work gloves, grimacing as he pulled the sap-caked, grimy fabric over his fingers, then left through the kitchen door and loped around the house. He'd left a pair of shears leaning against the building's wall, and he collected them as he passed.

The front porch was on the shaded side of the house, where dew still clung to the grass and the vines. The wooden porch wasn't small, but it had been crisscrossed with generations of vines that obscured the door beyond them, smothering the space like a living shawl.

Guy poked one of the curling, lime-green tendrils with the end of his shears. A drop of water fell off it. He considered leaving the porch until the sun could dry it out and warm him up, but that would mean either getting home late or letting it wait until he returned.

No, better I deal with it now. He dug around the porch's base until he found the base of one of the vines. Knotted tangles of toughened, cracked wood protruded from the decay-smothered ground. He put his shears around one of the stems and strained to cut it. Water rained down on him as the leaves shook. Shaking his head to get the droplets off, Guy grabbed the severed part of the vine with both hands and began dragging it away from the porch.

The wood groaned and cracked as its vines were torn free from where they'd tangled around other plants and the porch's supports. Guy staggered when it finally came free, then threw it behind himself and wiped grime and drops of water off his forehead.

The space was still a grizzled tangle of plant matter, but he'd removed a respectable section of it and could see the door more clearly.

A woman's corpse, twisted and enveloped by the plants, huddled in the porch's back corner.

CHAPTER 16

GUY YELPED AND JUMPED back. He had the impression of a grayed face, slack jaw, and empty eyeholes turned toward the sky, then he tripped over the vine he'd removed and tumbled onto his back.

What the hell? That can't be real—

His arms shook as they grasped at the vine to give him leverage to stand. Something feather soft and unpleasant ghosted over the back of his forearm. A small gray spider scrambled over him, its thread-thin feet waving erratically. Guy flicked his arm to throw it off.

His mind unraveled as it fought to make sense of what he'd seen. He rose slowly, afraid his legs would buckle, and edged closer to the porch. The shears had fallen near the front step, and Guy picked them up. He used their tip to push errant vines aside to give him a view of the front door and the small, shadowed alcove next to it.

Vines wrapped around a lamp attached to the side of the house. The leaves were no longer green but mottled grays and blacks as they withered and decayed.

Guy inhaled sharply and pressed a hand to his heart. The grayed leaves wrapped around the dead bulb created the impression of a distorted, bloodless face and empty eye sockets. The plants gathered below the lamp were reminiscent of a body, and stained wood behind it was just the right shade to mistake for dirty black hair.

It had looked so clear, though. His throat hurt as he tried to swallow around the lump in it. *This house is messing with my mind.* He'd never been a jumpy sort of person, but he guessed the isolation and claustrophobic spaces were making him see things that didn't exist.

The swing creaked as it shifted in the breeze. Icy sweat made Guy's arms and back itch, and he rolled his shoulders. He had an explanation for the figure he'd thought he'd seen, but it was still difficult to take his attention off that corner of the porch. The irrational, panicked part of his mind gibbered that the corpse would reappear if he looked away, only this time, its empty eyes would be fastened on Guy.

"Quit it." He smacked his shears at one of the vines as though that might quiet his mind. The swing continued to move, its mournful creaks beating at his sanity like a dripping tap. Guy tightened his lips and gave the porch's corner a final scan before kneeling to work the cutters through another of the thickened vine bases.

As the wood snapped in half, drops of water rained down onto Guy's arms and face. He shook himself to get rid of them, but some clung on—and then began to move.

Guy lifted his hand. Another two of the small gray spiders scuttled over his skin just above his wrist, and Guy smothered a grunt of disgust as he knocked them off. Tickles across his scalp told him more were in his hair. He beat his gloves through it, knowing that more grime and flakes of dried sap would tangle in there, then grabbed the severed vine and began pulling it away from the house.

A dozen spiders tumbled down the stem. Some bounced off his gloves, but others found purchase, clinging to him. Guy bared his teeth at them and pulled harder. Web threads glistened in the wan light. The vine broke free with a crash, all ten feet of it tearing away from the house in a solid mat, and Guy hurled it aside.

Hundreds of the gray spiders scurried off it and disappeared into the long grass. Their movement made the plant seem to shiver, and Guy beat the tiny arachnids off himself in disgust. They were everywhere. In his hair, on his pants, crawling under his shirt—

The anger burst through him like an inferno. A strangled scream caught in his too-tight throat as he smacked himself, tugging at the shirt harshly enough to tear through the cotton and leave bruises around his throat. He threw it aside, followed by the gloves, then he staggered back, panting and blinking through the haze of red blotting his vision.

"What the hell is wrong with you?" He hurled the words at the house, his voice hoarse and the syllables mangled. A string of spit hit his jaw. His heart felt about to explode from the strain.

Then the burning anger ebbed. Exhaustion flooded into its place, accompanied by intense shame. He bent over, hands braced on his knees, as he focused on breathing and waiting for his vision to return to normal.

I'm done here. The front door can wait for later. It's time to get home.

A gray spider skittered over his bare hand, its legs waving, but Guy didn't have the energy to flick it off.

"I promise you, I ate three solid meals a day." Guy stared at the pile of mashed potatoes his mother was heaping onto his plate. She'd cooked a feast for his return home, and by the way she fussed around him, she seemed to have assumed he'd starved during the time he'd spent at Rookward.

"You're looking peaky." Heather added another spoonful for good measure then settled back in her seat. "I worried about you the entire time you were there, you know."

Guy chuckled. "I told you I'd be fine. I didn't see a single bear."

"Hmm." Her lips tightened, and her eyes narrowed as she stared at her food.

Understanding hit him. *Mum must have learned about the*

murders when she called her uncle. That explained her initial reluctance to let him visit the house. She would have thought she was protecting him by not telling him about it…and in a way, she was right. Guy knew sleeping in the building would be a little more challenging now that he knew its history.

Guy forced extra brightness into his voice. He'd told her a highly sanitized version of his time at Rookward, omitting the visit from the teens, the face in the window, the spider-infested porch, the sleepwalking, and anything else that might give her a reason to worry. "I've made great progress. And the damage is really pretty minor for a place that's been empty for so long. It shouldn't take much to finish up."

Heather nudged peas around her plate. "How long?"

"A week, maybe two weeks. I'll pick up the supplies I need this afternoon and head back there first thing tomorrow." He'd done some mental calculations during the drive home. He should have just enough money left to afford everything he needed. Some of the rooms might not get painted, but that was less of a concern than repairing the structural damage in the family room and cleaning up the signs of neglect and age.

"You'll come back every few days, won't you?"

Guy hesitated. Driving from his home to Rookward took a bit longer than three hours; it wouldn't be economical to make the trip too often. On the other hand, the shower he'd taken upon arriving home was one of the most magical experiences of his life. He'd never felt so clean, and he was already dreading the coating of grime he would develop in the heatless, lightless house. "I'll play it by ear, okay? I want to stay there at least a couple of days, but no more than a week."

The peas began another lap around Heather's plate, prodded along by her fork. "Can you call me this time? I was worried."

He hated seeing the disappointment in her face. "I know, Mum. I'm sorry. The reception's awful, and my phone's battery dies within a day." He leaned forward. "How about this? I'll see if I can catch a carrier pigeon and send it to you. Would that help?"

She chuckled and finally stabbed one of the peas. "I like the white ones the best."

Guy joined her laughter, but his heart ached. He knew he was upsetting her by spending so long away from home, but he'd committed to the project. He'd considered the possibility of leaving Rookward half-repaired, and just accepting the drop in value, even though it would be steep. But he couldn't, not in good conscience. Another week or two of effort would be worth it.

"Hey, Mum, have you put any thought into where you'd like to move?"

She tilted her head to one side and continued to pick at her meal. "Oh, I don't know. Wherever you'd like."

An idea occurred to Guy, and he smiled. "How about somewhere near the ocean? You always liked it when we went there on holiday."

"Oh, I do!" She perked up. "Remember feeding the seagulls together? And chasing the waves! And buying the silliest hats we could find—"

"I got a giant pink one with Christmas baubles all over it." He chuckled. "While I'm away this week, I'd like you to picture your dream ocean home. Think about how close to the water you'd like to be, what your neighbors are like, how busy the area is. When I get back we can start looking for houses."

Heather's smile let Guy relax. He scooped potato into his mouth and cobbled together a mental list of errands for the afternoon. Buying supplies wouldn't take long, so he would have at least an hour to spare. He wanted to research the house's history. If Tiff had exaggerated her story, knowing the truth would put his mind at ease. If she hadn't…well, he doubted he could feel any more repulsed than he already did.

Guy glanced toward his mother's computer. It was set up in the living area, near the TV, and she would have a clear view of it from the kitchen. He didn't want her glimpsing any headlines over his shoulder, especially if she didn't know the gorier details.

The wall clock said it was just after two in the afternoon. The library would be open for another few hours. He needed to go into town for the supplies anyway, so it would be easy to stop by the library and log in to one of their public computers for a few minutes.

Guy finished his meal as quickly as he could without being rude then offered to help his mother wash up. She waved him off with a blithe, "Don't you worry about that, dear," so he kissed her cheek and promised he would be back by dinnertime.

CHAPTER 17

GUY KEPT HIS HEAD down as he entered the library. Virtually everyone had read about Savannah's accident in the local newspaper and seen pictures of Guy's face during the court case. Most had either forgotten the incident or were polite enough to ignore him, but the occasional narrow-eyed glare still followed his back whenever he ventured into the shopping plaza. At least they'd stopped throwing eggs at his house and stuffing threatening letters under the door.

The librarian watched Guy as he passed her desk. He didn't think it was his imagination that her watery blue eyes followed him a few seconds longer than other patrons, but he slipped behind a bookcase and settled in front of one of the computers. The seat hadn't been empty for long—it was still warm—and the browser opened quickly when Guy clicked on it. He typed Rookward's address and waited to see what it brought up.

To his surprise, the first result was a ghost hunter's blog. Guy tried not to scrunch up his face. He'd seen some strange things at Rookward, but nothing that didn't have a rational explanation. He started scrolling down to look at other links, but morbid curiosity pulled him back up. The page was titled "The Infamous Rookward Murder House—Proof of Ghosts?" Guy grumbled to himself and clicked on it.

Whoever had designed the blog deserved to be committed to a hospital for the aesthetically challenged, Guy decided. The page's background was black, and the text, set to a tiny font size, was gray. Floating specks of light began to dance across his vision as he tried to make out the words.

The article was well written, though, and Guy rested his chin on his fingers as he scanned the story. Apparently, the site accepted "tips" from people about local haunted locations, researched them, and then published the stories. Guy didn't know if the site owner was given to embellishment, but the account matched Tiff's story pretty closely. A family of five, murdered in their home by a demented stalker, then played with like human dolls for four days before police investigated. Amy's time of death was listed as 12:15 p.m., and Guy felt a twinge of unease as he remembered the clock in the guest room. *That's got to be a coincidence, surely? Or maybe someone tampered with the clock as a joke?*

Guy kept scrolling. According to the author, few people had visited the house—it was too difficult to reach for many casual haunting enthusiasts—but one person claimed to have heard slamming doors and refused to enter the building. At the base of the article was the promised proof of ghosts: a photo of Rookward, taken during the eighties according to its timestamp. The picture captured the house's front. The familiar vines crawled over the building's lowest third but didn't reach as high as they did in the present. A light glowed in one of the upstairs windows and silhouetted a tall, thin figure pressed against the glass.

The blog's author had helpfully zoomed in on the figure, blowing it up into a pixelated mess. It seemed to be a woman with long hair. Her hands were raised, splayed fingers pressed against the glass, and her head was tilted to the side as she watched the photographer.

Frowning, Guy slumped back in his chair. The image was unsettling, but he knew better than to think it proved anything. It could have been easily spoofed if the photographer's friend broke into the building, carried a candle up to the second floor, and posed for the picture.

That doesn't make sense, the cautious part of his mind whispered. *How did they get inside? The doors were both barred. Do you really expect them to climb through the broken window, over the exposed glass fragments?*

"Yes," Guy grumbled. One of his friends in high school had been a keen photographer. He'd gone to some crazy lengths to get the perfect picture, including lying in puddles and clinging to unstable tree branches twenty feet off the ground. Guy could easily imagine him scrambling over glass shards if it meant capturing a breathtaking photo.

And there was no denying the picture in the blog was

impactful. Guy moved the cursor up to the button that would take him back to the search results, but he didn't click it. The woman in the window was little more than a black smudge, but Guy couldn't look away. He hunted in the pixels for any hint of an expression. Was she angry at the intrusion? Would her mouth be open in a scream?

"Sorry, can I renew this?"

Guy's breath froze in his throat at the sound of the familiar voice. He rose out of his chair, his heart knocking against his ribs and sweat dewing over his palms.

Savannah stood at the library's desk, her long fingers clasped ahead of herself as she waited for the librarian to process her book. She wore one of her favorite dresses, a sea-blue affair with a simple brown belt. It contrasted with her hair and showed off the graceful curves of her shoulders and neck. She'd worn it on one of their early dates, and Guy's fingers burned as he remembered brushing them over the dress's neckline.

She hadn't seen him yet. There was still time to slip out of the library without her knowing he was there. But Guy's feet refused to move. A baby carrier rested beside Savannah. Lavender lace hid the contents, but Guy felt that if he could only take a step forward, he would be able to see—

"Thank you." Savannah took her book back and reached for the carrier.

Panic flooded Guy, and he moved backward in a frantic effort to hide behind the shelf. He hit the chair. It tumbled over, clattering against the desk and then the floor loudly enough to draw attention. Suddenly, it felt as if the whole world's eyes were on him: the librarian, the woman browsing for books, the man reading in a seat by the windows. And Savannah.

She was gorgeous, with soft skin, large doe-like eyes, and sweet lips that fell apart in surprise. Color bled out of her cheeks. Those long graceful fingers clasped together tightly enough to turn the knuckles white.

"I'm sorry." The words came out as a stutter. Guy raised both hands, palm out, and hunched his shoulders. He wished he could slink behind the computer desk, where no one could see him. "I was leaving. Sorry."

His legs felt like lead as they carried him past her, toward the door. Savannah moved half a step closer to the carrier. He didn't dare try to glimpse inside as he passed it, but kept his head down. The silence was agonizing, but the rushing in Guy's ears was so loud that he doubted he would have heard her even if she'd tried to speak.

He picked up speed as he passed through the library's doors, moving faster and faster until he was sprinting for his pickup truck. He threw himself into the driver's seat, smacked the button to lock the doors, then slammed his fist into the dashboard. The anger had come out of nowhere, scorching through him like an inferno. He thrashed about, kicking, punching, and screaming, feeling as though he were being torn apart and was unable to stop it. The fury spent itself in seconds, and regret poured into the hole it left. He collapsed into an exhausted heap over the steering wheel.

Why did I have to go to the library today? Tears stung his cheeks. Inhaling was painful, and he clenched his shaking fists until the nails bit into the palms. *Why did she have to see me? Why didn't I hide when I heard her voice?*

The final question was easy to answer: because he still loved her.

Guy rested his head back against the seat and focused on drawing air through his nose. From the little he knew about Thomas's stalker, Amy had been a sick individual. But in a strange way, Guy could empathize with her need to be close to the person she loved. He would be willing to sacrifice almost anything if it meant another chance with Savannah.

Guy fished the key out of his pocket with unsteady fingers and fit it into the car's ignition. He knew he was too shaken to be safe on the road, but all he wanted was to get out of town as soon as he could. Even returning to Rookward's melancholic halls would be preferable to bumping into Savannah again.

Soon, he promised himself. *Get home to Mum first, pick up the rest of your supplies from the next town over tomorrow, then go back to Rookward. The sooner you finish there, the sooner we can move somewhere far, far away.*

The car's tires dug through the long weeds that swamped the clearing. As he stared up at the house, Guy was struck again by how lonely Rookward appeared.

The myriad of black windows watched him from between the vines as he circled the house. The grime left over them looked like cataracts, blinding them, but somehow, they seemed no less perceptive. Guy parked his pickup truck in the same space as the day before, with its rear facing the kitchen door. As he got out, he noticed the vines were already starting to creep over the doorframe.

"Persistent blighters," he muttered. He'd only been gone for a day; he hadn't expected them to grow so much in that short amount of time.

He hadn't brought a padlock the last time, so he hadn't been able to bolt the door before leaving, but it stuck in its frame as though reluctant to let him back inside. He had to slam his shoulder into it to get it to swing open.

The shadowed kitchen was exactly how he'd left it. The knife still balanced on the edge of the chopping board. Cups and plates clustered at the base of the sink, and the ring of red lipstick almost appeared to glisten in the light, as though it had been planted freshly that morning.

I need to clear this room out. He shrugged out of his jacket and moved into the dining room. *It's got too much personality.*

Low crackles floated through the rooms. Guy frowned and tilted his head. His first thought was that the baby monitor had come back to life, but that was impossible—he'd thrown it out.

He followed the sound into the foyer then to the guest room. The radio beside the clock on the mantel was stuck on static. Guy pressed its button to silence it as uneasiness spread prickles over his arms. *I could have sworn it was off when I left.*

Sunlight pulled his attention toward the window. The woods, tangled and so old they looked weary, filled the view. He was struck by the feeling someone was there, watching him.

The teens didn't come back, did they? Maybe they wanted to see the house in the daylight. Well, it wouldn't bother me, as long as they don't break anything...

Guy blew a breath out. He wished he could feel the energy and enthusiasm he'd possessed on the first day at Rookward. The project had been full of possibilities then—the house had been full of secrets and surprises—but all he had left was deep, settled resignation.

Windows first. The weather report had predicted a storm late in the following day, and Guy didn't need the headache of additional water damage.

The afternoon passed slowly. Guy had brought a printed copy of a guide to installing windows, and he took his time fastening the fresh panes of glass into their frames. Tempered glass was expensive; the last thing he needed was to drop and break it before it was even installed.

First, he fixed the library's window, where the teens had broken in. He'd fastened a tarp over the opening before leaving, and it had thankfully kept the space clean while he was away.

The shelves only had a small cluster of volumes on them, and the effect was depressing. Guy couldn't stop thinking about it as he worked. The family obviously hadn't been poor to afford the house and its furnishings. *Maybe they weren't big readers. Or more likely, they hadn't stayed long enough to fully stock it.*

Rookward was sparsely decorated for a home of five. There were very few humanizing, distinct features except for the pictures in the stairwell and the sewing machine upstairs.

Maybe they'd only been here for a month or two before Amy found them. Or maybe she'd been stalking them for a while, and they moved out here to hide from her. That would explain the remoteness.

Guy stepped back from the installed window. It looked almost comical—clean, clear glass set into a worn-down frame and age-stained wall. Still, it was a good job. He flipped a cloth over his shoulder and grinned.

The family room wasn't anywhere near as easy. The frame had swollen from the water and wouldn't even fit the glass. As he sanded the wood down to fit the new glass panel, he was hyperaware of the bloodstained couch behind him. He knew it would be better to cut it up and throw it out the window, but he couldn't bring himself to touch it. Not yet.

While he was fitting the glass into the frame, the slow, drawn-out groan of a closing door made him flinch. He stared at the ceiling, daring the door to move again, but it stayed silent.

Guy thought of the photo in the blog: the woman pressed against the window, fingers splayed, face unreadable. He suppressed a shudder.

I'll be glad when I'm done with this house. He turned back to the window as a stress headache began to build behind his eyes. *It plays with my mind. I'm looking forward to the day that I never have to think about it again.*

CHAPTER 18

TICKLES OF FOREBODING CREPT across the back of Thomas's neck. He used a gloved hand to brush them away. He'd felt them so often over the last six weeks that they were becoming a nearly subconscious sensation.

Of course she's here. She's always here.

He kept his focus on the garden he was working in. There was no point in searching the forest; he never saw her. She was as good as a phantom in that regard.

A sound like breaking porcelain came from the house. Thomas dropped a handful of dug-up carrots into his bucket and searched the windows.

Louise no longer watched him from the kitchen, and the prickling unease intensified. That was one of the myriad of rules they'd established since the night Thomas had heard Amy in his children's room: doors had to stay locked at all times, and no one went outside without someone watching.

She probably went to check on Georgie.

Thomas pulled off his gloves and threw them into the bucket. The air was cool as day settled into evening, but already, sweat had built over his back. He hunted for signs of motion in any of the windows. A curtain shifted in Becca's bedroom. Two birds launched off the roof, spiraling toward the forest in a blur of wings and shrieks.

The kitchen window remained empty. Thomas crossed to it. The house's insides were dark. *Did Louise turn the lights off?*

His chest was tight enough to make breathing difficult. His fingernails itched, but he resisted the temptation to chew on the stubs. He pressed himself to the kitchen window.

The sink was still full of soapy water and dishes. Louise had started to wash up from dinner, but evidently, she hadn't gotten far. She'd finished frosting a chocolate cake, though, and left it, ready to cut, on the chopping board beside the sink.

"Louise?" Thomas rested his fingertips on the windowsill and craned his neck to see through the open door at the back of the kitchen. "Lou, is everything all right?"

He couldn't hear anything from inside the house. The suds in the sink were starting to burst, and among the cups and saucers was a broken plate.

His heart ached as he tried the kitchen door. It was locked, as it should have been. He jogged around the house to test the front. It was also sealed. Thomas rattled the handle then beat on the wood. He held still, ear pressed to the door, listening for any sign of footsteps moving through the building. He heard none. "Louise! Answer me!"

Thomas waited for only a beat before he leaped off the porch and kept moving. The setting sun cast a veil of oranges and bloody reds over the scene. He looked through the windows he passed, but they showed only his family home, undisturbed and empty.

"Louise!" His voice cracked. The prickles spread from his neck to his arms and his legs.

He stopped by the family room, where Louise lounged on the couch. Her hair was swept over one shoulder, and her hands were folded in her lap. Thomas drew a sharp gasp as relief overwhelmed him, but it didn't last for long. His wife wasn't sitting naturally; her head lolled to the side, and her back and shoulders held no tension, making her seem to crumple in on herself. Her eyes were open but staring toward the wall, unblinking. Thomas banged on the window. She didn't respond.

Then he noticed the vivid, dark patch of red spreading across the couch. At first glance, it looked as though she might have sat there specifically to hide it, but as he watched, it grew, creeping across the fabric.

"Louise!"

He snatched a rock out of the garden border and smashed it into the glass. Pain burned across his arm as the glass shards sliced into him. He wrestled his jacket off, wrapped it around his hand, and used the padding to knock the largest shards free. Then he vaulted through the opening, senseless to the cuts, and reached toward his wife—

Guy opened his eyes. His heart thundered, and sweat stuck his shirt to his back. He took a quick, sharp breath, surprised to find his lungs ached from lack of oxygen.

Another dream? It was clearer than the others and didn't fade as fast. He blinked and saw the image on the back of his eyes: a woman crumpled on the family room lounge, blood leaking from her back to stain the fabric. Shudders ran along his limbs, and he rolled onto his back.

The moonlight gave his room faint illumination, highlighting the age spots and cracked plaster. Guy traced the patterns as he waited for his heart to slow. *Obviously, the kids' story affected me more than I thought. My mind's trying to recreate the murder scene while I sleep.*

For a brief second, Guy considered the idea that he might be seeing the family's actual deaths. He'd heard of emotional imprints before. One of his college friends had spent some time experimenting with psychedelics and had tried to explain the concept to him while on a trip. A strong, emotional moment could leave a memory of itself in a location. Someone with the right disposition and openness—or the right drugs—could relive the experience.

Guy snorted and pulled the sleeping bag higher around his

shoulders. The theory was easy to dismiss. While his dream had recalled a series of clues scattered around the house, including the dish-filled sink, it had failed in a major area—the wife. In the dream, she had been plump, with sandy hair, unlike the taller, dark-haired woman in the family photographs.

Put it out of your mind. It probably happened nothing like that.

No matter how much Guy tried to force his body to relax, he couldn't get the tension out of his limbs. Adrenaline still beat through him. Every little sound in the house seemed magnified at night. The animal living in the attic had woken again, and it moved through the space above him, claws clicking on the boards.

Don't let your mind do this again. Guy tried flexing his hands, squeezing them into fists before slowly relaxing them again. *You've got a lot of work to do in the morning. Another night of broken sleep won't help anyone.*

Somewhere to his right, a door latch clicked. Guy kept his eyes closed, but he couldn't stop his eyebrows from pulling together. *Just the wind bumping an open door. Ignore it.*

The door's hinges creaked. The note hung in the frosty air, teasing Guy and wearing at his patience. *I'll have another search for the door tomorrow. It's obviously not the closet in the girl's room, and it's not the master bedroom. But I'll find it, and I'll jam it shut.*

A board creaked above his bed as the animal moved through the attic. Guy tried to imagine the beach house he and his mother would move to, somewhere with a pleasant, relaxed community. He would get a job. He would get his own place again. It wasn't too late to correct the path his life had taken.

Another floorboard flexed. The sound was subtle, but in the dead of night, it was all Guy could hear. A thick drop of some cold liquid landed on his cheek. Guy reached up to wipe it away. It was viscous and slimy, and it had a sour odor. He tried to squint at it in the dim moonlight. Then he looked toward the ceiling.

A long, bone-thin creature clung to the plaster above his head. Its body had contorted, its spine twisted into an unnatural loop, but the fingers digging into the ceiling were unmistakably human. Light glinted off two wide, dark eyes. The creature's head had been tilted back, far more than a human's neck could endure, to stare down at him between sheets of long, oily hair. Another drop of liquid fell from its gaping mouth to hit Guy's forehead.

He screamed and scrambled back. The sleeping bag clung to him; he fought it off, freeing his limbs, and pressed his back to the wall.

The ceiling was empty.

"What the hell?" Guy twisted, scanning the walls and the windows, hunting for the malformed woman. The dampness still clung to his face and fingers. "What the f—"

A door slammed. The impact shook the walls and made Guy flinch. He staggered to his feet and moved toward the room's exit. When he reached for the handle, he touched air; the door was already open.

I've got to get out. The thought pounded through his aching head, consuming him. He dashed into the hallway, eyes squinted nearly closed, and braced to feel the scratch of claws across his back. He barreled around the hallway's corner and toward the stairs. Static crackled from the master bedroom as the baby monitor came to life.

Impossible. I threw it out.

He took the stairs too quickly and stumbled on the last few. He hit the landing on all fours, dragging in ragged gasps and shivering. He caught the sound of feet being scraped along the second floor's hallway runner.

The front door was immediately ahead of him, but he still hadn't finished clearing the vines or removing the boards nailing it shut. He went left, into the dining room. The stairs creaked as something—or someone—came down them.

Guy swore under his breath. The dining room chairs were stained red. The fresh liquid glistened in the moonlight as it dripped off the backs and trickled onto the seat and legs. The stench turned his stomach. He clamped a hand over his mouth.

The dragging, scraping footsteps reached the base of the stairs. Guy pressed his eyes closed and squeezed around the bloody furniture, keeping his back as close as he could to the walls and cabinets. The kitchen door was almost within arm's reach.

"Thomas?" The voice, raspy and low, floated from the hallway. It sent a spike of fear through him. He reached the kitchen and ran through it, barely noticing the speckles of red gore dotting the sink's dishes and dribbling down the fridge. The back door was open. He leaped through and ran to this truck. He'd draped the tarp over its supplies without tying it down, but he didn't stop to fasten it. The equipment might fall out on the drive home, but he wasn't going to spend even another second on Rookward's ground.

He leaped into the driver's seat, slammed the door, and locked it. Then he reached across the seat and did the same to the passenger's door. His gasps echoed through the vehicle, deafening him to the outside world. He spared a glance at the house. Nothing materialized in any of the doors or windows.

Guy reached into his pants' pocket for the keys. It was empty. His heart dropped in a dizzying, lurching motion. He fumbled through every pocket on his person as he tried not to hyperventilate.

He knew where the keys were. He'd left them on the table beside his bed...on the house's second floor...the room farthest from the door.

"Damn it. *Damn* it!" He slammed his fist on the horn. The noise shocked a cluster of birds out of the nearby shrubs. They shrieked as they spiraled away, and Guy, panting and shaking, pressed his back into the seat. His vision had turned red. As he sat, it gradually faded to black, then cleared.

Rookward remained dark and silent, a massive but sedate monster crouched at his side. Guy flicked his attention between the black windows and open, empty doorway, but nothing disturbed its stillness.

The anger leeched out of him like a toxin. He regained control of his arms first, then his legs, and pulled them up onto the seat so that he could hug his knees against his chest. There was almost no room with the steering wheel in front of him, but he didn't care. He felt safe in the truck. The doors were locked. The only thing it couldn't give him was what it had been designed for: a way to leave the house.

CHAPTER 19

DAWN CAME SLOWLY. GUY had thought the fear and adrenaline would keep him alert through the night, but he managed to fall into a dozing state several times with his head rested against the door. When light finally bled over the horizon and spread across the thigh-high weeds and hulking building, he was freezing cold, stiff, and irritable.

Did last night even happen? If he hadn't woken in the pickup truck, he might have been tempted to imagine it was all a dream. The crazed dash through the building held all of the hallmarks of a classic nightmare; the unseen entity stalking after him, the surreal imagery, and even the way every chance to fully escape was foiled.

He felt calmer, at least. When he lifted his hands, they no longer shook. *I've got to go back in there. There's no way around it. I'm not going anywhere without the keys.*

He eyed the side of the building, idly wondering if it would be possible to climb the vines and break through a window, but he had to dismiss the idea. *This isn't the day to push my luck. I'd end up with a broken neck or worse.*

Guy inhaled to brace himself, then unlocked and opened the door. The car had been cool, but the outside air bordered on freezing. He wore only a shirt and pajama pants, and goose bumps puckered his skin.

He flipped the tarp off the back of the truck and found a hammer. It had a good weight, and he gave it a couple of experimental swings before turning toward the kitchen door.

Guy squared his shoulders and marched up to the still-open doorway. The sun was at a bad angle to illuminate the space, but even through the shadows, he saw the blood was no longer splattered across the fridge and sink.

"Hello?" He didn't expect a response, but he tried anyway. The house felt peaceful. He turned to the dining room and found the chairs just as clean as they'd been the previous day.

What happened? Did I have another one of those vivid, sleep-walking nightmares? Even if someone had been trying to prank him and put the blood there to scare him, they would have had no way to clean it off without also removing the layer of dust covering everything. Guy ran a finger through the gray powder. It clearly hadn't been disturbed in fifty years.

He chewed on the inside of his cheek as he moved into the foyer. He wasn't ready to fully drop his guard, but the tension was leaving his shoulders, and the hammer in his hand was starting to seem like overkill.

The stairs complained but carried his weight. He stopped on the landing and nudged the master bedroom door open. The space looked surreally calm in the morning. The spot where the bed had once stood was still empty, but the bedside table—which he'd left—held the faded blue baby monitor.

Guy stared at it, and suddenly, the hammer didn't seem so silly. "I threw you out. I remember…" He mimed the motion of dropping it into a bag. The memory had grown fuzzy, though. *Did I really bin it? Or was that a part of a dream?*

Why wouldn't I get rid of it? The thing creeps me out. It should have been one of the first items to go.

A floorboard shifted behind him. Guy backed out of the room and stared along the hallway. Shadows caught on the peeling wallpaper, making him see things that couldn't exist.

Keep calm. Get the keys.

He flexed his grip on the hammer and paced along the runner, keeping his footsteps slow and soft. Dust rose around him, catching in the light and tickling his nose. He scanned the children's rooms as he passed. The space that had once belonged to the girl caught his attention. He'd moved a crate in front of the closet to keep its door closed, but the crate had been pushed back and the closet hung open.

So it's this door, after all. He swallowed. *I definitely shut it. Did the teens come up here? I don't know how long they'd been in the house before I woke up. They might have snooped around a bunch of rooms. Maybe they returned the baby monitor, too?*

The idea was like a gust of fresh air. They could have found the plastic speaker in the bags of rubbish he'd thrown out and brought it back into the house. He had no idea why, but at least it explained how the little blue box was still in Rookward and not at the local garbage dump.

Guy turned the corner. The door at the end—the one leading to his room—stood open. As he stepped through it, his gaze was drawn to the ceiling.

The creature had hung above his bed, her fingers digging into the plaster. But the ceiling was spotless, save for the age stains and a crack in one corner.

That proves it. Last night was a hallucination. Some kind of bad dream that mingled with sleepwalking.

Guy placed the hammer onto the table and picked up his keys. He hadn't thought he was the kind of person to get scared by an old house, and he prided himself on his rationality. *So why am I turning to water in this place? I've been here for less than five days, and I feel like I'm going crazy.*

He tossed the keys up and caught them again. The truck was less than a minute away, waiting for him to rev its engine and speed through the weed-choked path.

Could I live with myself if I did that? He moved into the hallway and leaned against the doorframe. *I've paid for all of those supplies. The house is nowhere near livable in its current state, and, if the building's history is as widely known as Tiff suggested, it'll be tough to sell. Putting it on the market the way it looks now will only make that worse.*

An immense sense of exhaustion fell over him like a weighted blanket. He squeezed his lips together and paced along the hallway toward the girl's room. He shut the closet door and shoved the crate back in front to block it.

No more running away from my problems. I may not love this place, but I'm not in any sort of danger here. And as long as I'm not in danger, I've got to follow through on my commitments.

And I'm committed to Rookward.

Guy prepared himself a simple breakfast in the dining room. He heated the beans, knowing that something warm in his stomach would make the difference between a ghastly morning and one that was only moderately unpleasant. As he ate, he thought.

What's the chance that the teens are pranking me? Tiff had been nice enough, but Blake had come off as a bit of a jerk. It wasn't hard to imagine the pair of them sneaking back in the middle of the night to slam doors and move things around. Blake would probably find Guy's fear hilarious.

He pushed his plate aside and opened one of the plastic crates stacked at the end of the table. He'd brought a small bag of flour under the misguided assumption that he would feel like cooking on the portable stove. He opened its top and crossed to the kitchen door, where he scattered two handfuls of flour across the wood. It would be hard to see among the scuffed dust unless someone knew it was there and was looking for it, but it would show if anyone tried to walk through it.

Guy also put another patch of it at the door between the dining room and hallway. He made it large enough that it would catch any intruders but narrow enough that he could step over it without straining himself.

Satisfied, Guy dropped the flour back into the crate and finished his breakfast. As he ate, a faint droning noise intruded on his awareness. He frowned and tilted his head as he tried to locate it. It sounded like insects or a conversation heard from a long way away.

Or a TV...

He looked toward the family room. Even if the blocky TV still worked after all that time, it wouldn't have any electricity to power it. And yet, the crackle persisted. It really sounded like a talk show turned down to the lowest audible volume.

Guy moved toward the closed door. As he drew near it, individual voices became audible. A laugh track played. He twisted the handle and pushed open the door.

The noise ceased instantly. The TV's screen was black. The couch still stood at the opposite wall, waiting for its family to return to it for a night of entertainment.

Am I actually going crazy? Guy pressed his sleeve over the lower half of his face to protect against the mold. *Maybe the fungus is hallucinogenic. Can you be sent on a trip just by inhaling it? I thought psychedelic mushrooms needed to be eaten.*

He knelt in front of the TV and pressed his hand to the wooden side. It was warm. Not by much—just a degree or two hotter than the air temperature, as though it had been running for a few minutes and only just been switched off.

Guy pulled his hand back. His pulse throbbed behind his eyes, and the night of broken sleep had left him feeling sluggish and disoriented. He tried turning the TV's knob. It clicked around to different settings, but the screen remained dead.

Someone shifted on the couch behind him. Guy froze as the cushion squeaked. Shock kept him rooted to his spot, and he couldn't look away from the reflections in the screen. They were distorted and blurred, but he could identify four unique shapes on the lounge. The two largest cuddled together with a child on either side, watching him as though he were their entertainment.

It's not real. It can't be real. It's impossible—

One of the corpses sighed. The sound sent a rush of horror through Guy. He swiveled around. The couch was empty.

Guy stayed on his knees, his arm pressed over his mouth, though it was more in preparation of being sick than a fear of the mold. The room was empty. Quiet. Dormant.

What the hell is wrong with this house? He clenched his fingers into painfully tight fists. *What the hell is wrong with* me?

Guy blinked stinging eyes and stood. Burning, aching anger had returned to scorch his chest and fry his mind, but he had nowhere to direct it. *Are the teens here, pranking me? Is the mold sending me crazy? Have I been crazy all along, and the symptoms only decided to show themselves while I'm at Rookward?*

He wrenched open the window. Normally, he would have taken more care with the glass—it was brand-new—but right then, he didn't care. He grabbed the TV and hauled it off its stand. It was heavier than he'd expected, but he had energy to spare. He hurled it out the window. It made a satisfying smashing noise as it hit the yard.

Next, he went to the couch. The lumpy, discolored object still repulsed him, but he snatched up the decorative pillows and threw them through the window then went to work dragging the cushions out. The mold had wormed its way into the couch, and Guy knew he should have worn a protective face mask, but he was afraid if he lost his momentum, he would never get it back again. He settled for breathing as little as possible as he yanked out the first gummed-up cushion.

A massive red stain coated its back. Guy blinked at it as shock tore through the anger. It was like the bloom of gore he'd seen in the dream, where the woman had died on the couch. Only in reality, it was facing the wrong way, as though someone had turned the cushion around to hide it.

It doesn't matter now. Trying to regain his impetus, he pitched the cushion through the window. He kept his motions sharp as he tugged up a second cushion, but the fury had calmed, like a wave spent on a rocky shore.

All of the pillows and cushions were outside, leaving just the couch's base. Guy tried kicking it. The wood was spongy and decayed, and two woodlice scurried away from the impact site. Guy kicked it again, bearing his weight down with each motion, to break through the structure. It came apart in large splintered pieces, still bound together with the cloth covering. Guy tried to tear it with his hands, but was forced to admit defeat and go in search of a knife. He found himself a face mask and work gloves at the same time, and when he returned to dismantling the couch, it was with perfunctory efficiency rather than the earlier blind anger.

The room's atmosphere felt better once the couch and TV were removed. The mold had set up a camp under the couch, leaving a large, rectangular black patch to mark its location, but Guy felt less uneasy without the hulking thing filling the back wall.

He stripped the mask and gloves off as he went back to the dining room. He bagged them then went outside to wash himself as well as he could with the jug of water and a bar of soap.

What's happening to me? He lathered his hands an extra time and stared at the suds multiplying between his fingers. *Am I really having delusions? I can't believe I'm crazy. If I was going to lose my mind, it would have been after what happened to Savannah, not all of this time later.*

The swing was audible, even though the house hid it from sight. He stared up at the building. One of the upstairs curtains shifted in the breeze, its off-white fabric curling in a pattern that made it seem alive. He remembered the photograph showing the woman pressed to the window, face inscrutable as she stared down at the photographer. For the first time, he seriously considered the possibility that he was staying in a haunted house. A spike of terror rushed through him, making his limbs twitchy and his chest tight. Pushing the idea aside, he swallowed the tang of fear that had flooded his mouth.

No, he decided as he toweled dry. *Rookward isn't haunted, because ghosts don't exist. Which means I'm dealing with some kind of psychosis. I'll clean the mold out of the family room. If the visions persist after that, then I'll have to leave.*

That wasn't a pleasant thought. If something about the location was affecting his mind—and there was no way to remove it—then the house would be unsellable. Guy had precious little money left to spend on inspectors and specialist repairmen, let alone doctors. When he'd committed to restoring the building, it had been with the idea that he would pay for raw goods and learn whatever skills the job required. Outsourcing any part of the work was unfeasible.

Don't panic. Fix what you can, then reassess. Who knows, it might just be the stress getting to you. Except for that night you went home, you haven't had a full eight hours of sleep since you first came to this place.

As Guy reentered the house, a scratching noise echoed down the stairwell. He pressed his lips together tightly and exhaled through his nose. *If I'm going to remove stress, getting rid of whatever's in the attic is the first step.*

He hadn't brought any trapping equipment. Without knowing what kind of animal he was dealing with, it had been difficult to prepare. Whatever it was sounded heavy—possibly a racoon or a large stray cat. Guy tucked a roll of plastic bags and a flashlight into his back pocket and put on a fresh pair of work gloves. Then he picked up the crowbar and prayed that whatever lived above him wasn't in a bitey mood.

The trapdoor had been built into the second section of the

hallway, just past Guy's room. It had been painted to match the ceiling's plaster, but the dark outline was unmistakable. A small hole told him there had probably once been a stick to bring the trapdoor down, but he didn't know where to start looking for it. Instead, he dragged the chair out of his room and stood on it to reach the ceiling.

Dust rained over his head and made him cough as the trapdoor came loose. Guy hopped off the chair then squinted at the retractable ladder dropping out of the ceiling. It hit the carpet beside him with a heavy thud, and Guy brushed the last of the grime away from his face. Whatever lived in the attic had gone silent.

The rungs flexed under his feet. For a moment Guy was afraid they were too old and would break, but they carried him. He climbed slowly and cautiously, putting as much of his weight on his hands as he could. The hole above him was darker than the hallway. Guy shifted through the opening and blinked as he waited for his eyes to adjust to the attic's dim light.

CHAPTER 20

THE ATTIC SPANNED THE length of the house. Guy switched on the flashlight and panned its beam across the space. Rookward's attic had less clutter than the loft in Guy's childhood home, but boxes and old furniture had been stacked around the edges. The cobwebs that hung from nearly every surface created a bizarre blurring effect, as though Guy were peering through a light fog.

The ceiling was high enough to let him stand in the center, but it sloped down on both sides until he would have to crawl. Like he'd seen from the outside, a handful of ceiling tiles had come loose, but insulation packed into the space eliminated nearly all of the sunlight. Even with light coming through the attic door and his small flashlight, Guy had to squint to see the rafters and crates.

Plenty of places for a wild animal to hide out. He moved along the attic with slow, cautious steps. Every movement echoed back at him. He couldn't see any motion or disturbed dust, so he stepped toward the wooden crates grouped together in the center of the floor near the opposite side of the attic. At least two dozen of them were stacked nearly to the ceiling. Guy found not just their arrangement but also their position strange. They were made of cheap wood, which had decayed significantly. Splintered gaps in several of the crates let him glimpse inside, but as far as he could tell, they were empty.

What made them important enough to be separated from the rest of the boxes? And if they were important, why were they left so far away from the trapdoor?

He moved around the edge of the cluster and drew a quick breath. Hidden behind the crates, out of view of the trapdoor, were signs of habitation.

A thin mattress and blankets had been arranged in the center of the space. Both were grimy. They appeared to have been used often and never washed. The blankets had been left askew, and the pillow was bumped off the edge of the mattress, as though the occupant had left in a hurry.

Cans and glass jars, most opened but some still sealed, were stacked against one of the crates. Guy identified peaches, fish, beans, and soup. Behind them were boxes of cereal and long-life rations. The open cans were stained with the remnants of long-decayed food, and a musty, sticky smell made Guy gag. They looked as though they had been there since the sixties.

Papers had been stuck to the crates. They were lined up in orderly rows and arranged into distinct clusters with an unnerving level of precision. Guy had to sink to the ground and hold his flashlight up to the discolored sheets to read them. Many of the papers seemed to be journals.

11 March: Thomas finished his book. I waited until he was asleep then took it to read myself. It is healthy to share our interests. 12 March: Thomas washed his car. Children played nearby. He still looks for me in the forest, but he cannot yet seek me out; the whore is ever watchful. 13 March: The whore argued with Thomas. She is ungrateful. Fate was cruel to trap him with her. I wanted to go into their room and slit her throat while she slept, but I moderated myself. He is not yet ready for me.

"Wow." Guy ran a hand through his hair. *This must be how Amy was able to stalk him for so long without being caught. She wasn't in the forest. She was hiding in their own home, right above them. She would have been safe from the weather, and probably stole food from the house while the family was asleep. That's sick.*

Positioned among the pages were well-worn photographs. There was close to a hundred of them, all depicting the same man: brown hair, creases around his eyes, and a warm smile. A few showed him behind a desk in what Guy assumed was a bank office. Some were of him walking past buildings. Still more were of him in Rookward: Guy recognized the family room and the library.

In only two of the pictures—those taken in the bank—was Thomas aware of the camera. He was smiling in both of them. All of the others were candid shots, sometimes with leaves, fences, or dark, blurry shapes obscuring the camera's view.

She must have been stalking him well before what he endured in Rookward. A handful of the pictures had melting snow banked against the walls. Others showed deciduous trees full of leaves. *This would cover six months, at least.*

It hadn't been possible to see in the family portrait hung by the staircase, but Guy suddenly realized he and Thomas bore a lot of similarities. Their hair and clothes dated them to different periods, and Thomas seemed to have about a decade on Guy, but the resemblance was unmistakable, especially around the eyes.

Guy scanned the pages to find the last journal entry. The writing, which had been small and precise until then, became crooked for the final day. *April 19: He has promised the whore that they will leave. Is he truly choosing her over me? I can't believe he's sincere. I have sacrificed so much for him, more than he'll ever know. Now I will ask him to make a sacrifice in return. To prove his devotion. I will make him give up the whore and the whore's children. Only then can we be together. Only then can I show him the depth of my love.*

"Psycho." Guy drew back from the tableau of macabre words and photos. A dark spot on the attic floor caught his eye. Amy had whittled a funnel-shaped hole in the wood next to the mattress. It was nearly as large as Guy's palm at its opening but grew narrower until it was no wider than a fingertip. Guy had a horrible premonition about what the hole was for. He bent closer and squinted into it.

The hole opened into the master bedroom. He recognized the blue child monitor on the bedside table. The hole was positioned directly over where the bed had once stood, but if Guy twisted, its shape let him peer into almost any corner of the room.

They wouldn't have known. Guy's stomach flipped as he imagined lying in the bed and staring up at a black dot on the ceiling. It would have seemed like just a stain, or maybe a dark bug. Thomas would have had no way of knowing a woman was looking back down, studying him with a terrifying intensity.

Guy shuddered and looked away. Now that he was searching for them, he saw there were holes scattered across the attic—at least ten of them. *One for every room. She could follow Thomas anywhere he went and listen in on his conversations. That's horrible. It would be like having an extra member of your family you didn't know existed.*

Someone exhaled behind him. Guy twitched and turned to scan the shadows.

He couldn't see anyone among the cluttered furniture, but the sensation of being watched had fallen over him, and he couldn't shake it. "Hello?"

Guy didn't expect an answer, but he couldn't stop himself from speaking. The mattress had fifty years' worth of dust over it; no one had been here since Amy had made it her home. But at the same time, the attic felt less empty than when he'd entered.

Am I having delusions again? I should get outside, into fresh air. Guy turned toward the trapdoor—just in time to see it slam closed.

Guy gasped and stumbled back. His foot caught on one of the crates. He threw his arms out to catch his balance, and the flashlight slipped out of his grip. It clattered across the dusty floor as its light flickered then went out.

With the trapdoor shut, the attic was close to perfectly dark. Guy tried to swallow around the lump in his throat and stretched his hands forward. *It's all in your mind. It's got to be. You're safe. There's nothing here that you need to fear.*

Those thoughts didn't stop his heart from jumping and the hairs on the back of his neck from standing on end. As tightly as he clung to the belief that he was alone in the attic, he had no rational explanation for what had closed the trapdoor.

Guy shuffled forward, hands extended. His fingers touched one of the crates that circled Amy's home. Cobwebs stuck to him, and he had to repress a moan as he felt around the structure. The featherlight touches of tiny gray spiders crawled across his fingers.

Get downstairs. Get outside. You'll feel fine in a few minutes.

A heavy, scraping foot shifted across the floorboards. Guy threw a glance over his shoulder, but all he could see was a mosaic of dark shapes filling the room.

"Thomas." The name was like a whisper drawn from a dying person. Desperation filled the rasping voice. "Thomas."

It's in your mind! Guy's eyes were useless, so he squeezed them closed and relied on his touch to guide him forward. He was past the crates, but the webs still clung to his fingers.

The figure behind him took another step forward. Its feet slapped the dusty floor then scraped against it as they were dragged forward again. Guy hadn't noticed before how cold the attic felt. He blindly stumbled in the direction of the trapdoor.

"Thomas." The voice was closer than before.

A whine caught in Guy's throat. He clung to his rationality, repeatedly telling himself that the sounds weren't real, but the more he said it, the less true it felt.

He knew he had to be close to the trapdoor. He dropped to his hands and knees, feeling for it. Dust clung to the cobwebs and the spiders skittering up his arms as he sought a hinge, a ring, or the millimeter-wide gap that signaled his exit.

The shambling footsteps were almost on him. He could hear her breathing, sticky and quick, behind and a little to his right. *She's not real. She's not!*

Guy touched metal. He cried out from relief. His fingertips traced the shape of the hinges then felt forward toward where he knew the ring had to be.

A finger ran along Guy's cheek. He jerked back. The place where he'd been touched burned. A desperate need to scramble away from the unseen figure rushed over him, but he kept himself where he was, beside the trapdoor and the escape it promised. Guy threw both hands ahead of himself, panning them in a wide arc, and found the ring. He pulled it up. Light flooded through the opening.

Two bleached eyes stared out of the shadows across the trapdoor. They were round and unblinking, bordering on manic as the pupils traced over Guy's features. The intensity horrified him. He squeezed his own eyes closed and lunged, headfirst, through the opening.

CHAPTER 21

GUY REALIZED THE SEVERITY of his mistake as soon as his shoulders passed through the trapdoor. Rookward's ceilings were high, and it was a long way to the threadbare runner below—especially with his skull in line to break the fall. He stretched his arms out in a desperate attempt to stave off the impact.

Sharp pain shot through his leg. Something had caught around his ankle as he fell. The pain dug in, burning and making him cry out, then he slipped through and hit the ground hard enough to blot out his vision.

He blinked rapidly and groaned as he rolled onto his side. His bones hurt. His head throbbed. The cutting pains in his foot refused to abate.

Idiot! What in the hell possessed you to jump out headfirst? There was a ladder right there! It wasn't like you were in danger!

The belligerent internal voice faded into silence as Guy stared at the blood seeping from his leg. He tried rotating his ankle. Fresh pain flared, and with it came a stabbing, nauseating fear.

Something grabbed me as I tried to escape. It's not my imagination. A dream can't hurt me. Mental tricks can't cut my skin.

Guy tilted his head upward. He was just in time to see a long, sheet-white arm retract back into the hole in the ceiling. The disquiet transformed into a stomach-churning terror so intense that he thought he might pass out. Guy scrambled away from the attic ladder, only stopping when his shoulder blades hit the wall. His mind, still jarred from the drop and fogged with stress, fought to understand.

Was there really someone up there? It couldn't be—the dust hadn't been disturbed—

He touched his leg. Five long lines had been dug into the skin around his ankle, in a shape reminiscent of fingernails. Blood flowed freely.

It's not a dream. It hurts too much to be fantasy. Does this mean the other nights were real, too? Seeing that thing on my ceiling, hearing the TV, the footsteps and slamming doors and faces in the window—

His mind wanted to revolt. The implications were too awful to examine further. Guy shuddered then buckled over as he threw up. He wiped the back of his hand over his mouth and sucked air into his burning lungs. In among the panic, one thought rose to the front of his mind: *Get out. You've stayed far, far too long already.*

Guy pushed himself to his feet. The leg hurt, but shock helped to numb it. A weight in his back pocket told him he had the car keys, which was a relief. He kept the leg elevated and leaned on the wall for support as he limped around the puddle of what had once been breakfast and made his way down the hallway.

Above him, wood creaked. The thing—monster or human, he wasn't fully sure—followed his progress through the attic. Guy clenched his teeth to keep a panicked moan inside. *Is it really Amy? Did her ghost become trapped here after death, like Tiff said?*

He reached the staircase. The steps were harder to navigate without jarring the cut leg, but he used both hands to stabilize himself. Guy knew he was leaving a trail of blood over the carpet and floorboards, but he didn't care. He no longer wanted anything to do with the cursed building.

An upstairs door groaned open. Guy braced himself, but he still flinched when it slammed. He focused on each new step and how much closer it brought him to the outside world. He reached the foyer and passed over the flour barrier into the dining room. Guy stopped just long enough to grab the hammer out of one of the crates, then he continued into the kitchen, across the second flour line, and outside.

The cool afternoon air burned his lungs, but he kept drawing in huge gulps of it. Shivers ran through his arms as the shock-induced adrenaline lent him excess energy. He pulled his keys out of his back pocket as he neared the pickup truck.

I should have done this long before now. He jumped into the driver's seat and locked the doors before wiping the sweat out of his eyes. *I was an idiot to ignore what was happening. At least it's not too late to escape.*

His right leg ached, but he knew he'd be able to drive well enough with the left. He put the key into the ignition and turned it. The pickup truck's engine clicked but didn't start.

Sickening fear latched on to Guy's heart and dragged it into his stomach. He licked at dry lips and tried again. The clicking repeated.

Come on, girl. You've never failed me before, no matter what sort of awful conditions I put you through. Show me some of your fighting spirit.

Tk-tk-tk-tk-tk. The noise matched Guy's thundering heart. He bit his tongue to stop from yelling as the familiar burning sensation replaced the lump of ice in his stomach.

It was startling how quickly the fear mutated into anger. Guy smashed a fist into the horn then shoved the truck's door open and lurched out. His vision blurred as he yanked up the hood of the car, bent over the engine, and gripped the metal frame so harshly that his hands hurt. He waited for the fury to abate. When he blinked, his vision had cleared enough to let him see what he was doing.

There was no smoke, which was a good sign, but at first glance, Guy had trouble identifying the parts of his engine. A large, lumpy gray shape rested over the instruments. As Guy stared at it, the shape started to undulate.

"What the hell?" He reached out. As soon as his fingers touched the shape, it whirled into motion, breaking apart and spreading like a sentient liquid. A scratchy sensation covered Guy's hand. He yanked it back to stare at the fuzzy gray shapes crawling over it, then he choked on a scream, thrashing his arm to free it.

Gray spiders had grown a nest over his engine. They'd stayed clumped together and, once disturbed, swarmed through the pickup truck's belly, spiraling across the metal and plastic in a frenzy of waving legs. There must have been more than ten thousand of them, all smaller than a penny but daunting in their quantity.

Guy tried not to gag as he rubbed his arm to get the spiders off it. He'd seen plenty of them around the house, but his nerves were raw and his patience thin. He hopped around to the truck's back and grabbed one of the large jugs of water.

Carrying the weight with a compromised leg was a challenge, but desperation propelled Guy toward the car's hood. He yanked off the jug's lid and poured its contents over the spider nest.

A frenzy of gray gushed out of the truck's underside. They washed around Guy's shoes and disappeared into the long grass. He didn't stop pouring until the jug was empty and only a handful of stragglers remained. Then Guy threw the jug aside, breathing heavily, and returned to the driver's seat.

He refit the key into the ignition. Then he released a muffled, miserable groan as the familiar *tk-tk-tk-tk-tk* filled the space.

I've only been parked here for one day. That's not enough time for a spider nest to be laid, mature, and hatch. Unless the nest has been in the engine for a week or more, and I just didn't realize…but if that were the case, wouldn't I have cooked the eggs while driving around?

Guy flopped back in the seat. A single tiny gray spider descended from the windshield and hung off its web in front of Guy. He twisted his mouth at the waving limbs.

165

It's got something to do with the creature in the attic. Guy turned to the building. He couldn't see movement in the open door or any of the windows. *Whatever it is…it's not human. It can change things. Create hallucinations. Make electronics work again. If it really is Amy, is it her ghost? I thought spirits weren't able to touch physical objects.*

Guy looked down at his leg. The cuts were clotting, but blood still soaked his sock and trickled down into his shoe. He would need to bind it somehow. His first-aid kit was in the kitchen. He could take his shirt off and tie that around the cuts, but that left him open to infections. And if he couldn't get his car working that day, falling into a feverish delirium at Rookward could easily kill him.

He twisted the key a final time and listened to the motor click futilely. Then he swore, released his grip on the steering wheel, and unlocked the car doors.

CHAPTER 22

HIS LEG HURT MORE as the adrenaline faded. Guy set his jaw as he limped toward the kitchen. Shifting the hammer from hand to hand, he peered through the doorway. The house was almost disarmingly calm. Still, Guy waited for nearly a full minute before hopping over the undisturbed flour patch.

I've been here for a bit more than three full days. It didn't hurt me until I went into the attic. It probably won't try to do anything as long as I stay on the lower level. Right?

Guy was acutely aware of how vulnerable the injured leg made him. Walking was hard enough; running might prove impossible. He moved with agonizing slowness as he shifted from the kitchen to the dining room. Even with the window clear of vegetation, the interior of the house felt too dark. Guy lit the gas lamp and set it in the center of the table. Then he shuffled through his supplies to find the first-aid kit.

He'd brought the kit from his family home. His expectations of Rookward were so tame that he'd only checked it had plenty of bandages and a packet of painkillers before packing it. As he dug through the supplies, he found there wasn't any antiseptic.

Mum must have taken it. He chewed on his lip as he fought the rising panic. Then an idea occurred to him. Moving so that he didn't turn his back to any of the doors, he fished the bottle of brandy out of the box. It had been half-drunk, but there was plenty left to disinfect the scratches.

Guy boiled some of his bottled water while he collected clean cloths and selected bandages. Every few seconds, he paused to listen and watch the open doorway to the foyer. There was no sign of company, but that didn't do much to comfort him. He eased the shoe off as carefully as he could. Blood had pooled in it and mixed with the water he'd splashed while cleaning out the car. A single gray spider crawled out from among the shoelaces, and Guy squashed it against the table with a grimace. He set the shoe aside and worked the sock off next.

The woman—he'd started thinking of her as Amy—had torn through the sock. He discarded the bloodied item then worked on cleaning the cuts.

Five slices circled his ankle where she'd tried to drag him back into the attic. When he poured the brandy over them, they stung so badly that Guy had to bite his forearm to keep silent. He was shaking and sweaty by the time he cleaned the wounds with the boiled water, then he gave them a final wash with the brandy for good measure and bandaged them. A soft groaning noise behind

Guy made him startle, but it was only the kitchen door swinging on its hinge.

The cuts weren't too deep, but they were long and would need stitches once he was back in civilization. He'd dripped blood all through the building in his desperation to escape. But thankfully, he didn't feel dizzy. He hoped that meant the blood loss wouldn't impair him too badly. Guy's mother had been a nurse before she married his father, and he remembered her telling him that the body needed a lot of water to regenerate blood. He drank deeply from the jug then set about packing up his kit.

The house had remained quiet while Guy worked. He stayed alert for the scraping, dragging footsteps, but as far as he could tell, he hadn't been followed.

She can look into all of the second-floor rooms but not downstairs. Guy still couldn't keep himself from scanning the ceiling for tiny, dark holes, but he couldn't pick any out among the myriad of aged stains.

Guy threw out the dirty water then leaned against the table as he assessed his situation. Tiny patches of blood had begun to ooze through the bandages, but he didn't think the foot would start bleeding seriously again as long as he didn't use it too much.

The sun was close to the skyline, which gave him less than an hour to work on the car while he could still see. He knew his way around mechanics, but the pickup had never failed him before, and Guy still didn't know what had broken. He didn't like to think about what he would do if the truck couldn't be repaired. Guy fished a rain jacket out of one of the crates and fastened it around the injured foot to protect the bandages, then he hopped back outside to the car.

He'd brought a lot of tools for the trip, anticipating having to sand wood, drill holes, and plug leaks, but car repair tools weren't among them. Guy was reduced to hunting through the engine with his hands and a spanner.

Dozens of the little gray spiders still clung to the motor. They'd begun to weave webs through the area, and Guy used the spanner to knock most of them loose. He couldn't immediately see any cause for why the car wouldn't start, unless the spiders had somehow gotten inside the pipes and clogged the engine. That was a grim thought: he had no way to dismantle it without seriously damaging it.

Guy muttered under his breath as he went over the engine. Again and again, he traced the cables and checked the connections, hoping he'd missed something obvious. Every ten minutes, he went back to the driver's seat and tried the key again. The result never changed.

By the time blood-red stains began spreading over the horizon and the forest's shadows stretched halfway up Rookward's walls, Guy was forced to admit defeat. His shoulders ached, and his head hurt as he sat on the edge of the vehicle and stared at his hands.

Where does this leave me? My phone will be thoroughly dead by now. Without a car, there's no way to leave.

If he took too long to come home, his mother would worry and either look for him or call the police. Guy groaned and pressed his hands over his face. He'd told her his stay at Rookward might last as long as a week. That left six days before she would become alarmed enough to talk to someone.

I could walk... He peered over his shoulder toward the forest. Hobbled as he was, it would take at least three hours to reach the main road. Then he would either have to walk to town—a half-day trip on foot—or pray a car happened to be traveling along the remote street in the middle of the night.

And that was if he didn't get lost. His mind conjured up an image of stumbling through the tangled underbrush, blind in the depths of night, while wild animals chattered around him and the freezing air bit at his skin. He repressed a shudder. Traveling through the day would be safer, but it would mean spending another night at Rookward.

Is that a better choice than risking the woods, though? That... thing...has disturbed my sleep every night since I arrived here.

The sun had almost fully disappeared behind the trees, and the temperature was dropping. Rookward's driveway had become so overgrown that Guy doubted he could follow it at night, even with a lamp. It also opened him up to the risk of hypothermia, something he would be increasingly susceptible to after losing blood.

Rookward's going to be the safer option. He almost laughed at that idea, but the thought of spending the night in the house with Amy made him feel too sick for mirth. *I've gotten through three nights here, carried by ignorance and probably a bit of luck. I can manage a fourth, surely?*

Guy slammed the hood. It was tempting to sleep in the vehicle's truck bed, outside the creaking house and away from its bulging-eyed host, but that wasn't a practical option. The pickup truck was only a few paces from the house, and he would be vulnerable, even if he brought enough blankets to stay warm. He limped around to the truck's back and hunted through the supplies stacked there.

He still had plenty of food, but washing the spiders out of the engine had wasted a full jug of water, which left Guy with what remained in the jug in the dining room. It didn't have much liquid left. If Guy ended up being stranded at Rookward for more than a day—either because of an infection or something more malevolent—he would run out.

The weather forecast had promised rain that night. Guy re-arranged the supplies in the back of the pickup so that they were all gathered toward the edges, then he fastened down the tarp so that it had some slack. He put a small wrench in the center of the tarp to weigh it down, creating a bowl to gather water. Then he picked up the hammer, rolled his shoulders, and limped indoors.

No way in hell did he intend to sleep upstairs. It was too close to the attic's opening and too far from the door. Instead, Guy fashioned a bed for himself in the kitchen, using spare clothes and blankets, then stood back to admire his work. Guy hadn't brought enough spare blankets to protect against the kitchen's tile floor. He would be cold without the insulated sleeping bag.

How dangerous would a trip upstairs be? He peered through the window. Night had set in, and birds chattered in the trees as they settled. Guy thought of the attic trapdoor. He'd left it open. *I've only ever seen her in lightless places. If Amy becomes active in the dark, she could come crawling out of the hole any minute.*

On the other hand…if she's physical enough to cut my leg, she wouldn't be able to move through walls, would she? I could shut the trapdoor. Find a way to lock it. Then she'd be trapped up there.

Just the idea of going upstairs made stress squeeze around Guy's heart, but he'd already made the choice to spend the night at Rookward, and that meant securing it to the best of his abilities. The trapdoor opened downward, which meant he would need something to jam against it. He shuffled toward the family room. During the trip home, he'd bought new planks to cover up the holes in the floor. They were long but thin, so Guy gathered three of them, duct tape, the lamp, and a saw. Then he turned to the staircase.

Dragging the wood upstairs with a bad leg took Guy more time than he was comfortable with. Panting and sweating, he took a minute to lean against the wall in the upstairs hallway while he gathered his energy.

A muted crackle came from the master bedroom. Guy nudged the door open with his elbow and extended the lamp inside. It was empty, but the baby monitor sat on the bedside table. It looked too innocent. Guy waited, but no other noise came from it. He lifted his gaze toward the ceiling. There, above where the bed had been, was the tiny, pencil-thin hole in the plaster. It really did look like a stain or an exposed screw head. Guy shut the door then lifted one side of the planks.

He dragged the wood down the hallway, letting the back ends of them scrape over the runner and shred the decayed fabric, creating a cloud of dust. He stopped before the hallway's bend and peered around the corner. The trapdoor hung open like a gaping mouth, its insides impossibly dark. Guy lingered by the corner for a moment, waiting for the blanched-white arm to extend out of the hole. When it didn't, he squared his shoulders and moved forward.

Getting the wood around the bend took a lot of maneuvering. Though Guy struggled to keep his movements as quiet as possible, he ended up having to scrape one end of the wood against the peeling wallpaper to get them all into the second stretch of the hall.

A floorboard flexed above Guy's head. He froze, scanning the wooden ceiling for any of the tiny holes, but it was hard to find them among the wood's natural color variations. He swallowed and quickened his pace toward the trapdoor.

Guy stopped underneath it, dropped two of the wooden boards, and used the third to bump the trapdoor shut. The latch made a faint clicking noise as it caught. He knew it would be wishful thinking to imagine that would be enough to keep Amy in the ceiling; she'd come down on previous nights, after all.

The chair Guy had initially stood on to reach the trapdoor waited beside him. He dragged it directly under the opening then arranged the wooden planks around it to form a tepee shape. He shuffled the boards in so that their tops converged neatly in the center of the trapdoor.

Something scrabbled at the wood above him, and the planks shuddered downward. Guy had a split second to choose between running and standing his ground. His first impulse was to move back, but then he imagined lying awake at night, knowing Amy could be anywhere in the house, maybe as close as the next room, maybe watching him sleep. He grabbed the planks, shoving them back into place and bracing them the best he could with one hand. Then he reached into his pocket for the tape.

The trapdoor shifted down with a harsh scrape. Guy caught a glimpse of pale skin and staring eyes before he forced the planks back. The trapdoor banged closed again, and Guy gripped the loose end of the duct tape between his teeth and yanked a length free. He wound it around the planks, his fear pushing him to move too quickly and leave slack in the tape.

The creature banged on the trapdoor again. A grunt escaped Guy as he fought to keep his supports against the door. He kept winding, and gradually, his loops became tighter and straighter. He released his grip on the planks to crouch down and bind the wood to the chair. By the time the tape ran out, he had what he hoped was an inflexible structure. He stepped back, panting, and stared at the trapdoor.

Whatever waited above didn't try to escape again. Guy swallowed and wiped the back of his hand across his mouth. He shook his tepee structure. It barely shifted an inch. There would be no way to remove it without cutting the tape, and it blocked the only way out of the attic—he hoped.

Guy's legs were shaking, and fresh pain stung the cut ankle.

He limped into the bedroom and grabbed his sleeping bag and blankets off the ground. His initial plan had been to collect the bedding and get out as soon as he could, but he couldn't stop himself from glancing toward the ceiling.

It took a moment of hunting, but Guy located the tiny black hole above the desk. He was faintly surprised he hadn't seen it while staring at the ceiling during his sleepless nights—but he supposed he hadn't been searching for it then.

Guy threw the blanket over his shoulder and bundled the sleeping bag under one arm as he moved into the hallway and shuffled toward the stairs. Even with the supports in place, he didn't feel completely safe turning his back on the trapdoor.

This is enough, isn't it? I should be safe for tonight, shouldn't I?

He reached the hallway's corner and paused, one hand on the flaking wallpaper, to watch the brace and trapdoor. He hated not having any answers to his questions.

The holes in the roof tiles aren't large enough for a human to fit through, and I didn't see any other doors in the attic.

But then, I don't know the house like Amy does.

He'd been worrying at his lip, and the chapped skin ached. Guy dug his nails into the paper until it crinkled, then he limped toward the stairs.

This has to be enough. Because I don't know what I'll do if it's not.

CHAPTER 23

GUY SAT AT THE table until well after midnight. He was exhausted, but his nerves wouldn't let him sleep. He couldn't stop his mind from scanning through the building and searching for ways the creature could escape from the attic. He'd done the best he could to secure the plank-and-chair structure but couldn't disperse the niggling worries that Amy was stronger or more cunning than he'd given her credit for.

He poured the last of the brandy into a glass and sipped it. There wasn't enough left to get him drunk, but he hoped it would help steady the shaking in his limbs and the throbbing in his chest.

The storm had rolled in a little after eleven. He saw it before he heard it; lightning flashed through the windows, painting weird shadows over the wall and making Guy flinch. Thunder followed. It shook the air, and Guy squeezed his eyes shut as though that could block it out.

Rain came not long after. It was heavy and harsh as it came down in thick drops, but the drumming noise actually helped to soothe Guy. He sat for a while, keeping his mind empty as he watched the drips trail down the window, then he rose and shut the door to the foyer. He'd left it open to help him hear the noises from deeper in the house, but Amy had remained silent. He propped a chair under the handle, hoped it would be secure, then moved into the kitchen and toward his bed.

Guy lined up both the hammer and crowbar within easy reach then put the lamp, still lit, on the ground where it would illuminate most of the room. He shuffled into the sleeping bag but left it unzipped in case he needed to race for the door.

The pain in his leg had dulled to a soft ache, and the blankets felt warm. Guy held onto his pillow as he watched the intermittent lightning brighten the kitchen's window. He only counted three flashes before he was asleep.

Thomas couldn't breathe. Blood stained his fingers; the sticky texture felt as though it might never leave him. He stumbled through his house as he tried to call for his children. *Becca. Dan. Georgie.* The words came out as hoarse gasps, so faint that even he couldn't hear them above his pounding pulse.

He saw Louise's face every time he blinked. Her dead, staring eyes. Her lips, drained pale. The way her head had drooped when he'd shaken her—

"Dan!" He started up the stairs. "*Becca!*"

Amy had gotten into the house. He didn't know how—not when they'd taken so many precautions and always locked the doors—but she'd managed it. She was an infestation, a rot that had set in and would never leave. His legs were weak, but desperation and fear spurred him up the stairs to the second floor.

The baby monitor played muffled sounds in his bedroom. A woman crooned a lullaby; Thomas recognized the tune he sang to his children every night. His throat was too tight to allow breathing. Spots of terror-induced white burst across his vision as he pushed on the door to the children's room.

Amy leaned on the edge of the crib as she sang into it. Blood glistened in her hair, dripped down her face, and even discolored her teeth as she turned her smile toward him.

Small figures lay in the beds. They didn't move. Thomas's strength gave out, and he crumpled to his knees. "No—not my children—please—"

"Shh." She pushed away from the crib and swung her hips as she waltzed toward him. "It had to be done, dear one. They were distracting you from *us.*"

Thomas couldn't tear his gaze away from Dan's hand, hanging limply off the edge of the bed. Red liquid dripped off the fingertip. A sickened whine rose in Thomas as his vision blurred.

"Thomas, Thomas, shh." She knelt in front of him, pressing bloodied hands to his cheeks as she tried to pull his attention back to herself. "I'm here for you. I've *always* been here for you."

"Don't touch me." Thomas was disgusted to hear the words

come out as a moan. He tried to twist out of Amy's grip and reached toward his children. "Don't touch me. I need to—my *children*—"

Amy's smile twitched. Her grip tightened, keeping him immobilized. She tilted her head to one side, and her wild black hair fell across one eye. "They're gone, but I'm here, my darling. I love you. We can be together now. This is what we always wanted, wasn't it? It's what you promised me back then. Don't you remember?"

He remembered. The too-warm afternoons when she'd slipped into his office and they'd locked the door. The sweetest kisses. The feel of her flesh against his. The promises she'd wrung from him—promises to leave his wife, to choose her over his family.

And he also remembered the way she'd grown twisted as soon as he tried to stop the affair. The illicit honey was sweet, but it came with a price too high for any sane man to pay.

"You repulse me."

Her smile was falling, and it spurred Thomas to add venom to his words.

"You were a toy. Easy to manipulate. Easy to lie to. I never would have given up Louise, not for *you*. You're deluded if you think I ever cared for you."

Amy's face twisted into grimacing anger. A sharp pain burst through Thomas's chest. He looked down; their kitchen knife dug deep into his stomach.

"Mine." A string of spittle fell from Amy's bared teeth. She pulled the blade out and returned it home with each repetition of the word. "Mine. Mine. Mine. *Mine.*"

Thomas tried to speak. Blood flooded his tongue and dribbled over his lips. He scrabbled for purchase, and his fingers grasped at Amy's shoulders and neck. The anger in her face softened as she leaned closer, her words slowing into a soft lullaby. "*Mine. You're mine. Mine.*"

She kissed him. Blood ran between their lips. Darkness swirled across the edges of Thomas's vision. He felt cold. So horribly, achingly cold…

Guy snapped awake. He was blind, but his breaths were sawing rasps in his ears. He clutched at his chest and stomach, afraid of finding the punctures he'd felt in the dream, but his body was still whole.

No moonlight made it through the clouds. Guy held his hand above his head, but he couldn't see the fingers. His lamp had gone out—probably from lack of fuel. He felt as though he'd slept for a long while, but no sign of morning cut through the abysmal black outside.

A deep, permeating foreboding soaked through Guy. He rolled onto his side and wrapped his arms around his chest. *You're safe. She's trapped in the attic. She can't get out.*

A floorboard creaked near the opposite side of the room, below the window. Guy twisted toward it, but the world was black. He thought about searching for the lamp, but even if he found it, the fuel would be nearly impossible to identify by feel in the boxes of supplies. *It was just the house flexing. That's all.*

Rain continued to drum at the windows and the walls. Guy couldn't stop his ears from searching for human sounds through the drone any more than he could stop himself from hunting for shapes in the black. He was desperate for morning, but it felt as though it might never come.

As the seconds morphed into minutes, Guy slid back into sleep. Uneasy dreams tugged on the edges of his awareness. He imagined a light moved past the window, illuminating the staring eyes just inches from his face, but the image faded before he even had a chance to feel fear. Thunder rumbled, so close that it seemed to shake the building's foundations.

When Guy woke, the storm had finally calmed and morning's light brightened the edges of the sky. He rolled onto his back and blinked at the ceiling. Ghastly tiredness dogged him, but he didn't want to stay inside the building any longer than he had to. He pressed his palms into his eye sockets and braced himself to get up.

The air was bitingly cold without the blankets around him, and Guy shuffled into the dining room to bundle himself in layers from the crate of spare clothes. His foot was stiff and aching, and sharp pains radiated toward his knee with every step. He blew on his hands then went to start the portable cooker to boil the last of his water. If he was going to hike back to civilization, he would need all the caffeine he could get.

With the pot on the stove, Guy hopped back toward the kitchen. The light was insipid and hard to see by, but the rain had cleaned some of the grime off the windows. Guy glanced toward his bed and froze.

He hadn't seen them in the dim light while waking, but white marks spread across the walls and floor around where he'd slept. He scanned the doorway; the flour he'd laid down was scuffed in a wide arc. *Don't panic. You walked through it yourself multiple times.*

Guy swallowed as his eyes drifted higher. The white marks spread over the walls and onto the ceiling. His heart turned cold. *She wasn't trapped after all. How long did she spend watching me sleep?*

His attention shifted toward the window. A tree had come down during the storm. Guy rubbed his hand over his chilled nose as he shuffled to the window. The huge oak with the swing had fallen; he could see the wooden board lying beside the felled boughs, the ropes limp and tangled in the overgrown lawn. Guy was surprised to feel a twinge of remorse. The creaks had tormented him, but the tree had been magnificent, and he imagined the swing had been loved at one time. The yard felt sadder and lonelier without it.

Something metallic glinted a little past it, near the forest's edge. Guy frowned and leaned closer to the glass. The shape looked like a car.

That's not possible. Is it? Has someone really come to Rookward? Why didn't I hear them?

He passed through the kitchen door as quickly as his bad leg would let him. The clouds were breaking apart. Guy inhaled as golden sunlight hit his face; just being out of Rookward's encasement felt like breathing properly for the first time. And yet, the sense of dread that had dogged him through the previous night remained. He rubbed at the prickles creeping over his arms as he waded through the weeds toward the car.

As he neared the vehicle, recognition hit Guy. It was the same sedan the teens had driven. The car was old and worn, but details like the clean windows and new seat covers showed it was cared for. Guy came to a stop at the driver's side and peered through the glass. A purse lay on the passenger seat, but otherwise, the sedan was empty.

"Tiff?" Guy stepped back and faced the house. He scanned the windows, but the only light in the building came from the stovetop in the dining room. He raised his voice into a bellow. "Tiff!"

I thought I dreamed about light coming through the window. It must have been her car headlights. Why would she drive out here in the middle of the night? And where did she go? The only way into the house is through the kitchen, and she would have had to physically step over me to get past.

Guy chewed on his lip, staring across the yard. His attention was pulled toward the tree that lay there like a fallen giant, its massive, knotted roots torn from the ground in an explosion of dirt. Something colorful rested under the trunk. The prickles of disquiet that had bothered Guy through the morning turned into a painful, terrifying buzz.

CHAPTER 24

"TIFF" GUY RAN, IGNORING the pain in his leg. The patches of loosened dirt made him stumble as he rounded the exposed roots to reach the trunk. His vision blurred as though his brain refused to accept what the eyes were capturing. Flashes of a pink cardigan and blue jeans mixed in with flesh-colored tones. Soaked into them was a deep, dark red.

Guy stopped a few paces away from the girl and dropped to his knees. The image was so unnatural that Guy had to blink and look a second time to make sense of what he was seeing.

Everything above Tiff's waist had been crushed under the tree's trunk. She was face down, her legs twisted at an awkward angle, one sneaker half off her foot. The weight of the tree must have been immense; the trunk lay flush with the ground, and Guy knew there wouldn't be much of Tiff's torso and head left even if he managed to lift the oak off her. One of her arms poked free, its bloodless fingers curled toward the sky. Guy reflexively reached out to hold it. The skin was ice cold and damp from the rain. A miserable, wailing cry choked in his throat.

This can't be real. She's not dead. It's got to be a joke—a prank—

"Blake!" Guy swung away from the tree to scan the yard and the house. A circling bird's mournful cry answered him.

He slumped back and pressed his hand against his face. Nausea rose, but there was nothing in his stomach to bring up. Instead, tears flowed.

Guy sat next to Tiff's body for a long time. Rain drizzled over him, freezing him. He kept his fingers around her hand. The skin gradually warmed where he held it until it was only a few degrees lower than his own temperature. Guy kept waiting for the fingers to move, to squeeze him back, to reassure him that he'd misunderstood and everything was really all right. They stayed stiff and unresponsive.

Leaving the girl seemed ruthless and insulting. But as the sun moved higher and shifted the angle of the shadows around him, Guy was forced to pay attention to reality. Thoughts came back like scattered fragments of a shredded book, and he slowly pieced them together.

She brought a car. I can leave. Bring the police back, get them to help me move the tree off her—

He stumbled to his feet and limped to the sedan. It was parked not too far from the tree. He could picture Tiff battling her way across the yard during the storm and not even hearing the crackle as the roots were torn out of the ground.

This wasn't a coincidence. He reached the car and tried the handle. It was unlocked. *That creature—Amy—she did this.*

He moved into the driver's seat. Sitting in the dead girl's car, claiming the same spot she must have taken hundreds of times, made uneasy prickles crawl over his back, but he couldn't pass up the chance of escape.

The keys weren't in the ignition. Guy picked up the purple satchel bag on the passenger seat and opened it. The bag was cluttered with receipts, ChapSticks, pens, tissue packs, and a folded-up gossip magazine. He emptied it and went through every pocket carefully, but the keys weren't there, either.

A moan built in Guy's chest. There was only one other place they could be, but the idea of raiding the dead girl's body was enough to make his hands shake.

Do it now, before you lose your nerve. He jumped out of the car and flinched as the impact jarred his foot. He returned to the fallen tree, mouth dry and heart aching.

"I'm sorry." She couldn't hear him, but speaking helped assuage the guilt as he knelt at Tiff's side. "You didn't deserve this. I'm so, so sorry."

Her clothes were still wet from being soaked in the storm. Guy tweaked the edge of her cardigan up to expose the jeans' pockets. Something white poked out of one. Guy tried to pull it free but felt the slight give of damp paper tearing. He left it and instead felt around her other pocket. It was empty.

"Where did you put your keys?" Guy frowned and tried to peer under the tree to check if she had any pockets in the cardigan. He couldn't see her upper half at all, just a collage of fabric, blood, and fractured white bones. He pulled back, the sickening image making his stomach lurch, and cold sweat spread over his body. Her cardigan material was knit, and he was fairly sure it wouldn't have embellishments or pockets. Guy sagged back onto his heels. "They've got to be *somewhere*."

Birds chattered in the trees above his head. Guy ran a hand through his hair then returned to the white paper in Tiff's pocket. He had to ease it out with excruciating care, but even then, he managed to pulp one corner of it. The shape turned out to be a letter folded in thirds, with a second sheet of paper tucked inside. Guy shuffled away from the body and carefully unfolded the first page.

Tiff had written on it with a purple pen. The ink had bled in parts, but Guy could still make out the message. The lump in his throat tightened as he read.

Hey Guy,

I'll leave this note under your door so I don't wake you up again. I've had to sneak out, otherwise my parents wouldn't let me come here. I found some stuff about the house's history and thought you'd be interested. Blake doesn't like talking about these things, and my friends think I'm weird when I bring it up, but you seem cool. Maybe we could meet up some day and have coffee if you want to chat about it or whatever? Text me.

Following that was a number. Guy frowned at the message. It was a lot of work for a teenager to sneak out of her house after midnight and battle a storm just to get a note to him. Then he noticed the way she'd signed her name—a tiny heart replaced the dot above the *i*.

Did she like me? He tried to think back to the first night Tiff had visited. He didn't remember picking up on any signals. On the other hand, Blake had glowered at him with more venom than Guy thought he deserved.

Guy wished he could feel flattered, but instead, he just felt sick. It was his fault Tiff was dead. Not directly, maybe—but if he'd never come to Rookward…

If I'd never come to Rookward, a lot of things would be different. Guy scratched his fingers through his hair then shivered. *First Savannah, now Tiff. Am I cursed to hurt the people who care about me?*

His mouth tasted unpleasantly tacky. He remembered he'd left the pot of water on the stove. He didn't want to abandon Tiff, but he could very easily burn up his supplies and shelter if he left it. He refolded the wet note around the second sheet of paper and lurched to his feet.

Guy gave the tree an experimental push. It was massive, and he couldn't see any way to get it off Tiff. The idea of letting birds come down to peck at her was sickening, so Guy took off his jacket and draped it over her legs. It was poor protection but the best he could manage.

The dusty, dim inside of Rookward squeezed Guy as he

reentered the building. He kept his eyes roving across the space and his awareness on high as he moved through the kitchen.

No bubbling sounds came from the dining room, and when he entered, he knew why. The pot had boiled dry, and the metal was starting to turn red. Scowling, he switched off the portable heater and left the pot on it to cool.

That's the last of the clean water gone, then. But at least it rained last night. Guy slumped against the dining room wall. He unfolded the wet note and laid it on the table to dry. The second sheet was made of thicker printer paper. Guy flattened it out.

It was a photocopy of a newspaper article. Four smiling faces looked out of a large photograph heading the article. Thomas, his wife, and his two eldest children posed for the picture. The title read "House of Horrors."

Guy scanned the article. It covered the finding of the Caudwell family after their deaths. It lined up with what both Tiff and the website had recounted: the police had found Amy with the corpses at 12:15 on a Wednesday. There was evidence that the bodies had been dressed in different outfits and moved around the house, as though Amy had been playing with human-sized dolls. One of the later paragraphs caught Guy's attention.

It is believed that the killer, Amy Westmeyer, was the daughter of the senior partner at the bank Caudwell worked at, Westmeyer & Rogers. A source at the bank claims that Amy visited the establishment frequently and often spent time speaking with Caudwell. The police investigation is ongoing.

Guy rubbed at the back of his neck as he laid the second sheet of paper out to dry beside the first. *So my dreams really were accurate. Were they emotional imprints? I guess if I can believe in ghosts, I can believe in those, too.*

He bent closer to the photocopy. The family was all familiar, but one party caught him by surprise. The mother was plump and had sandy hair, the way he'd seen her in his dreams. He pushed away from the wall and moved into the hallway. He kept his ears open for the dragging footsteps as he cautiously climbed the lowest part of the stairs to reach the photographs of the family gathered on the couch. In this version, the mother was tall and had dark hair. A small smile curled her lips, accentuating her high cheekbones and shadowed eyes.

"No way. She didn't..." Guy ran his fingertip over the rest of the group. None of them smiled. Their eyes didn't quite meet the camera, and their bodies seemed oddly slack. Guy turned the frame over and pulled out its back. A second photograph was hidden behind the first.

He'd found the original photo. The image showed the family in exactly the same position on the living room couch, but they were alert and smiling. The sandy-haired woman sat close to Thomas's side and held his hand. The girl had kicked one foot up, obviously more interested in her boots than in the picture being taken. They seemed happy.

Guy glanced between the two photos. He remembered the candid pictures of Thomas in Amy's attic hideout. *She must have had a Polaroid camera or something similar. She didn't like having*

Louise in the pictures, so she reshot them after the massacre, with herself as Thomas's wife.

The pictures didn't feel clean. Guy dropped them and rubbed his hands on his pants. A slow, groaning noise came from beyond the upstairs landing as one of the doors shifted open. Guy swallowed and backed down the stairs.

My car won't work. I can't find Tiff's keys, and I have no idea where else I should search for them. That means it's time to start walking. This place is going to kill me if I don't get out—and soon.

CHAPTER 25

GUY CHANGED INTO DRY, warm clothes from the supplies in the dining room then dug through the crates until he found a cloth bag, which he shoveled full of canned food. He could wait until he was away from the building before eating. He also undid the plastic he'd fastened around his bandaged leg and managed to ease a boot over the red-tinted bandages. Finally, he took one of the empty water jugs and carried it outside to fill from the reservoir he'd created in the back of the pickup truck.

He tried his hardest not to look toward Tiff's car or the tree blocking her body from sight. Instead, he focused on his own vehicle. As he'd hoped, the tarp was nearly full with water. He scooped handfuls of the liquid into his parched mouth and drank as much as his stomach could handle. Then Guy dunked his plastic jug into the pool and half-filled it. It was a fine line between weighing himself down and bringing enough to guard against the possibility of becoming lost.

I've got food and water and enough clothes to keep me warm. Guy rotated his foot. It ached but not like it had the day before. *There's nothing else I need to bring, is there?*

He tilted his head toward the sky. Most of the morning had already been lost. Not wanting to delay any longer, he hitched the bag onto his shoulders and stepped toward the driveway.

As he neared the forest, the birdsongs and scraping sounds of branches shifting together enveloped him. He stepped past the line that marked the original clearing's edge and let the tension ease out of his shoulders and neck. He was away from Rookward, and that was all he cared about at that moment.

The path was easier to see than he'd expected. The weeds and shrubs were still flattened where his pickup and Tiff's sedan had crawled over them. He set up a brisk pace, attention fixed on the ground ahead of him as he followed the tire tracks.

Soon he was warm enough to take off his jacket. Perspiration trickled down his neck, so he drank more of the water to lighten his load. *The trip to the main road should only take two or three hours. Then, if I'm lucky, I'll be picked up by a passing car. I could be back at home before night.*

The tire tracks began to fade. Guy frowned in the muted light as he tried to follow them, but the patches of flattened weeds were appearing less and less close together. Soon he couldn't see them at all.

This can't be right. Guy turned back to the way he'd come, but he could no longer see the path between the trees. Panic tightened his chest. The ground was too uneven, and the gaps between the trees were too narrow to drive a car through. *How did this happen? I was following the tracks—I didn't let them out of my sight.*

He took a deep breath. The scent of moist, loamy earth filled his nose. The bird chatter was a cacophony. It took several minutes to calm his heart and slow his mind.

I'm going to be fine. Even if I've lost the path, I'll just need to keep walking in the same direction. Eventually, I'll reach the road. I just have to move in a straight line.

The low branches and crawling vines were disorienting, and the sun was too close to overhead for him to orient himself, but he pointed his feet in the direction he believed would run parallel to the driveway and kept moving forward.

The ground grew increasingly uneven. Guy's pace slowed to a crawl. His foot was aching, and he regretted not spending the extra minute at Rookward to pack painkillers.

It can't be far now. Time seemed distorted. He couldn't tell how long he'd been walking—hours, possibly. He was panting and stumbling but didn't want to stop for a rest until he'd reached the main road. Guy used his arms to carry part of his weight on the branches as he progressed through the woods. The plants had grown stiflingly tight. Almost every step involved climbing over fallen, moss-coated logs, sliding down inclines, or clambering over vines.

Guy tried to silence the anxious what-ifs running through

his mind, but every time he thought he'd squashed them, they resurfaced. *What if I'm going in the wrong direction? What if I can't find the road?* He tried to remember what he'd read about survival situations. They said not to move around too much, that the chances of being found were better if you just camped where you were. Except in his case, no one was searching for him…and wouldn't be for at least another five days.

I should have brought more water. His throat was dry, but he didn't want to drink any more until the thirst became more pressing. Tiny insects fallen from leaves and vines crept across his skin, but he didn't have the energy to brush them off.

Between the swaths of muted browns and greens, he caught sight of a gray shape. The stress in his chest loosened, and he quickened his pace.

A stone fence cut through the trees. Guy recognized the lichen-clogged stones; it was the same fence he'd torn the gates out of. He got close enough to press a hand to the cool stones then peered down its length. He couldn't see the opening in either direction. *I must have been farther from the path than I thought.*

He backed up. The fence was only slightly higher than his head, and plants clustered close to its edge. He chose a young, twisting oak that seemed promising and pulled himself onto the lowest branch. His ankle burned when he put his weight on it, but he kept moving upward until he was high enough to drag himself onto the top of the wall. He paused there for a moment, breathing deeply, then looked over the opposite side.

The view wasn't encouraging: there was no sign of the road,

only more woods exactly like the forest he'd already passed through. He carefully raised himself to standing. The aged stones were crumbling and unsteady under his feet, but he stood as tall as he could. No road or path was visible in either direction.

That's all right. The lane has bends in it; it's not surprising that it doesn't run against Rookward's wall the entire way. I can't be far from it.

He tossed the bag over then crouched and lowered his legs over the side of the fence. Even dipping himself as low as he could, there was no avoiding a drop. The impact jarred him and set his foot burning again. He rolled onto his back and scrunched his face until the pain subsided, then he snagged his bag and hopped to his feet again.

He considered following the fence in hopes of finding the gate, but he didn't know which direction he needed to go or how long it would take. If he chose the wrong path, it could strand him in the forest until after nightfall. He didn't think the lane could be far away, though. He faced straight ahead and pressed into the forest.

The ground tended downhill, which Guy was grateful for. He kept his attention roving over the terrain as he moved, alternately watching his step and hunting for gaps in the trees. He let his mind fall quiet and simply focused on the movement of his legs and the dragging of his lungs. He'd lost track of time when exhaustion finally brought him to a halt. He blinked at his surroundings.

The sun was no longer high in the sky. The beams that managed to fight through the canopy were slanted at a steep angle.

Guy shuffled to a cool, mossy trunk that had fallen in his path, and exhaled as he sat on it. His sore legs relaxed. Guy checked the injured ankle; blood seeped through the bandages but not enough to be a serious problem. It ached like hell, though.

I've been walking for hours. I can't have missed the road, could I? He twisted to search behind himself, but the view was nearly identical to the one ahead.

His throat burned almost as badly as his eyes. He opened the bag and drank the last of the water he'd brought. His appetite had vanished, but he made himself eat a can of cold soup. He'd left early enough to assume he would find civilization before night and hadn't packed any kind of bedding material or any way to light a fire.

Animals moved through the bush around him. They sounded large. More than once, he imagined hearing dragging footsteps, but when he looked in their direction, there was nothing but vegetation.

What the hell went wrong? Guy dropped the empty soup can then held his head in his hands. *Do I turn back and try to find the wall again? Or keep walking and hope I find a residence? Tiff lives…* lived…*around this area. There's got to be other houses, as well.*

He rubbed at his aching eyes then tucked the soup can and plastic jug back into his bag. They were empty, but he already had enough guilt on his conscience without adding *litterer* to the list. His legs were like lead, but he made them stand and hitched the bag over his shoulder.

Someone sighed behind him. Guy twisted but couldn't see

anything. His mouth tightened in disgust. *Just keep walking. That's all you can do. You'll find someone eventually.*

He continued to follow the slope down. His body wanted to take the hike slowly, but the sun was growing ever lower, and Guy's urgency increased in tandem with the beams' slant. Daylight began to turn into twilight, and the visibility reduced. Without contrast, the forest blended into one tone, and Guy kept stumbling over rocks and potholes.

Then he heard water. It started as a faint murmur, but as he quickened his pace, he made out distinct sloshing, bubbling noises. He broke through the trees and found himself on a riverbank.

The water was at least twenty feet wide and moving quickly. Even in the last moments of daylight, Guy could see the miniature rapids and eddies. He bent over with his hands braced on his knees, physically and emotionally exhausted, his stomach in knots.

That's it, then. I definitely missed the road. How far into the wilderness am I now? Which is the stupider choice—continuing on in blind hope or turning back and enduring the freezing night?

A light blinked on across the river. Guy's heart lurched, and he took an unsteady step forward. Trees and darkness obscured the glow, but it had to be man-made. *A camp? A house? Either way, it means people.*

"Hello!" Guy bellowed the word, but the forest muffled it just as thoroughly as it absorbed the dying light. He stopped at the edge of the river. The water moved quickly; he didn't like to think of the odds he would be facing if he tried to ford it. But not far away, a tree had fallen over the stream. It was old and decayed, and the trunk was breaking apart, but Guy thought it would still carry his weight. He went to it and struggled through the wild tangle of dried roots to clamber onto the trunk.

The tree groaned under his weight and bowed closer to the water. Guy took a series of quick, deep breaths then began crawling across it on his hands and knees. The moss was slimy under his fingers, and insects crawled out of the holes he punctured. Guy grimaced against the sensation and focused on the golden light flickering between the trees.

Wood creaked then fractured. The tree dipped farther into the river, and Guy felt the cold water snatch at his leg. He threw himself forward, scrabbling up the trunk, then toppled off it as the force of the river began to drag it down.

Guy landed on the riverbank. He blinked up at the canopy then exhaled a thin cheer. He wanted nothing more than to lie there and rest, but the light was too close to ignore. He forced aching muscles to pull him to his feet. The fallen tree had broken in half and become jammed in the riverbed, with water rushing over the center where his weight had cracked it.

He adjusted the bag around his shoulders and fixed his eyes on the light again. Night had stolen away even the disorienting twilight. He had to use his hands to feel the path forward. Guy kept his focus on the light, even when trees blotted it out from sight and anxiety squeezed his heart. It was like a lighthouse guiding a battered, leaking ship home.

Then the woods thinned, and Guy broke through into a clearing. The light was coming from a window. The two-story house stood in the middle of a clearing that hadn't been mown in a long time. As Guy shuffled toward it, he recognized the house's silhouette. The peak of its roof, its vine-strangled walls, and the glint of moonlight off the tall windows were all familiar...

Guy came to a halt, his stomach dropping and his mind numb. He was back at Rookward.

CHAPTER 26

GUY STOOD IN THE lawn as shock slackened his limbs and numbed his mind. He turned to his right. Tiff's car waited a dozen yards away, its hood reflecting the moonlight behind the fallen tree. His own truck would be behind the building.

That's impossible. I only crossed the wall once. I only crossed the river once! How could I have looped back on the same building? And what's causing the light?

The last question prompted Guy to move. The glow was coming through the dining room windows. It was bright, had a gold tint, and offered the impression of warmth. Guy was freezing. He shuffled forward, resentful that he had to return to the building but starved for choices.

The back door still stood open. Leaves and bits of dirt had blown in and mixed with the remnants of the flour. Guy waited on the threshold, listening, but there was no sign of Amy. He dropped his bag and continued into the dining room.

Someone had lit the gas lamp. Guy checked it and found it had been given fresh fuel. He ran his fingers through his hair.

This ghost, woman, creature—Amy—she must be doing this. She somehow twisted me back to the house. She lit the lamp to guide me inside. She broke my car and hid Tiff's keys…all because she doesn't want me to leave.

So then, what does *she want?* Guy pulled a chair out and collapsed into it. A headache throbbed in the back of his eyes. *I look a lot like Thomas Caudwell. Amy loved him. Does she expect me to take his place?*

He resisted the temptation to drape his torso over the table and cry. Despite the aches, the headache, and the way stress made his limbs throb, he couldn't afford to rest. Resting meant giving Amy the upper hand, and she already had too much of an advantage.

But what can I do? Following the driveway to the road didn't work, and it's a fool's hope to believe I can revive the car. Tiff's keys are missing, and short of scavenging through the yard for them, I don't know where else to look. All of my options involve walking in circles…literally.

Tiff's letter had dried on the table. The paper was warped in creases, and as Guy's mind tried to pick through his problem, he let his gaze drift over the purple-ink words.

Maybe we could meet up some day and have coffee if you want to chat about it or whatever? Text me.

He sat a little straighter. *Did Tiff bring her phone with her?* It hadn't been in her pockets, and he didn't remember seeing it in her purse, but then, he had only been searching for keys.

Guy shot out of the chair and grabbed the lamp. It was night, but in a twisted way, he actually felt safer outside. He hopped back into the thigh-high weeds and sought out the sedan.

The car loomed out of the darkness, and Guy hurried forward to wrench open its door. The contents of the purse were still laid over the passenger seat. Guy left the lamp on the ground outside then stepped into the car to rest his legs. He sifted through the trinkets, but there was no phone.

"Damn it." *Did Amy hide it, like she did with the keys? If she died during the sixties, she shouldn't know how cell phones work…*

Guy put his hand on the door to push it open again. His fingers touched something solid and metallic in the little pocket below the handle. Guy pulled the object out and exhaled a laugh as he stared at a cell phone.

It was a newer model compared to his, but the screen had already developed a crack. In a wave of hope, Guy checked both the driver's and passenger's door pockets for the keys, but they weren't there. *Still—a phone's a step forward. As long as it turns on…*

The mobile came to life when he pressed the power button. Guy watched the logo fade in and out, then his attention darted to the top bar as soon as the screen lit up. The phone had forty-two percent of its battery left but no bars.

Guy chewed on his lip. He stared at the screen, willing it to develop a signal, but the bars didn't change. He tried dialing a number just in case. It wouldn't connect.

A hand slammed on the car's window. Guy yelped and jerked back. Amy stared in at him with wide, unblinking eyes. She tilted her head to one side. The hand, its fingers painted red with blood, slid down the glass. Then she faded. Like evaporating mist, she was gone before Guy even realized what was happening.

His heart throbbed. He'd bent as far away from the door as he could but reached forward and pressed the button to lock it then did the same to the passenger side.

She's getting bolder. Sweat beaded over his back and face. He clutched the precious phone to his chest as he twisted to peer through the car's other windows. When he turned back to the passenger door, the bloody streak left by Amy's hand was gone, too.

So she can touch the physical world…but only for brief moments at a time? That means she can hurt me again. It also means the boards against the attic door are useless. Not that that's a surprise.

Guy could see Rookward through the car's windshield. He couldn't stomach the idea of returning to the building. The car wasn't necessarily safe, but at least it wasn't the house. His thirst could wait until sunrise, Guy decided. He tightened his jacket around himself and settled back to spend the night in the dead girl's car.

He dozed erratically. Rain started falling in the early hours of the morning. Guy initially hoped the noise would be soothing, but it wasn't. In among the water's gentle taps was something harder: fingertips knocking against the sedan's hull. They tapped around the car's outside, running along the sides and across the roof, a plaintive request to be let in. The lamp outside the door cast elongated shadows across the car's ceiling. Guy initially tried to search for Amy among the shadows and falling rain, but when he couldn't see her, he pressed his eyes closed. His legs cramped, and it was nearly impossible to get them into a position to relax them.

The rain continued into the morning and obscured dawn. Guy, exhausted, finally fell into a proper sleep. The tapping followed him into his dreams.

"Are you enjoying yourself, my dear?" Amy tightened her fingers around Thomas's hand. They sat in the family room as they watched the static play over the TV. It was after midnight, and rain drizzled through the broken window, creating rivulets across the wooden floor. Thomas didn't reply, but he seemed happy, as did their three children lounging on the floor ahead of them.

Lightning burst across the sky and brightened their room for half a second. Amy drew a slow breath and held it as the thunder shook the air. The lightning reflected off her husband's clouded eyes and the teeth in his slack jaw. His gums were turning black. Amy wished they wouldn't.

She preferred spending time with her family at night. The TV's static cast a gray pall over the room but didn't properly light it. It was better that way, when they were all safely cocooned in the house's shadows. It made it harder to see the dried blood coating her dear husband, the green-gray shade his skin had turned, or the way his eyes were shriveling in his skull.

"Don't worry so much. I'll keep you safe." She rubbed her thumb across his limp fingers as she answered his unspoken question. "You know I can. I removed that whore of a woman, like excising a tumor from your life. She made you miserable, didn't she? You argued constantly. Unlike us. We never disagree. It's proof we were meant to be together, don't you think?"

The static crackled. Water continued to spread across the floor. It was soaking into the girl's dress, but Amy didn't want to have to get up and move her again. The girl's slack features didn't register any alarm or distress, so Amy supposed she enjoyed playing in the puddle.

She kept the children for Thomas's sake, but she hoped he would soon grow tired of them, like she had. Then she could move them into the attic, where she'd hidden their whore mother. It would be easier now that they were no longer frozen by rigor mortis.

"I hope we can stay like this forever," Amy whispered. She passed an arm around Thomas's shoulder and pulled him closer, so that his cheek rested against her hair and she could tuck her head into the nook below his chin. His skin was cold and starting to bubble with decay, but she didn't mind. He was with her. That was the way it was supposed to be.

Guy gasped as he broke out of the sleep. His legs ached from the awkward position he had them in. His cheeks were cold, and when he touched them, he found tears. He scrunched his face up and used the backs of his arms to wipe away the wetness.

The tapping noise that had dogged him through the night had finally ceased. Water created a beautiful pattern as it ran down the windshield. Guy stared at it as he waited for the tingling numbness to leave his leg. The clouds muted the sun, but it was day, and he vastly preferred day to night.

Guy had dropped the mobile during his sleep. He felt around the car's floor, between a long-lost french fry and a candy wrapper, until he found it. He powered it on. The battery was down to thirty percent. A single bar appeared. Guy bolted upright, but before he could press a button, the bar vanished.

"No, come on! Don't do this to me!" He stared at the phone, willing it to regain its bar, but it wouldn't budge, not even when he moved it into different locations in the car.

Still, a vanishing bar is better than nothing. It might just need the rain to clear. Or maybe it will work if I can get it to a higher elevation.

Guy glanced at Rookward. He didn't want to think about returning to the upper floors. But if it let him make a call…

The phone fell to twenty-eight percent power. He turned it off to preserve its battery. Then he shuffled closer to the windows and peered out.

The weeds surrounding the house had been weighed down

with water. They shifted in the wind, but as far as Guy could see, nothing lurked among them. The lamp he'd placed outside the car had run out of fuel during the night but remained where he'd left it.

He opened the door and barreled out. The rain wasn't heavy, but it was consistent, and drops trickled down the back of his neck and wormed into his hair to chill his scalp. Guy grabbed the dead lamp and moved toward the back of the house. He tried his hardest not to look at the tree covering Tiff, but he couldn't help himself. Her hand was still visible through the rain. Flies swarmed around it, and Guy tasted bile.

Despite the cold and the wet, Guy stopped for a moment beside his pickup truck and shoveled handfuls of water into his mouth. The pool had started to collect drowned bugs and small leaves, but he was too tired to care.

Back inside the house, he shook himself dry in the kitchen. He spent a moment refueling and relighting the lamp. The house was dim on a good day, but with cloud cover, it felt as if it were still night. He couldn't see any sign that his possessions had been disturbed, so he turned on the phone and checked its bars a final time. No signal.

"All right." Guy set his jaw and tucked the phone into his breast pocket. "Up we go."

The stairs seemed steeper than he remembered. Guy climbed carefully, sticking close to the wall and alternating his attention between the top landing and the open doorways he could see in the foyer. Glass crunched under his shoe. He looked down at the photo frame he'd dropped; the two pictures lay beside each other. Amy's cold little smile appeared to be intended for Guy. Someone had scratched over the wife's face in the second picture, digging the pigment out of the photo until it was just a block of white. Guy shuddered and kept moving.

As he reached the top of the stairs, the master bedroom door groaned open, as though inviting him inside. Guy stopped dead. The bed, which he remembered dismantling and throwing out the window, was back in its place. He gazed toward the baby monitor just as it crackled to life. The sound of footsteps echoed from the device. Guy shrank away from it then moved to the next room along, the girl's.

Rebecca, he corrected himself. *I know all of their names. Louise, Dan, Becca, and Georgie. The dreams have to be replays of what happened to them.*

The closet's door was open once again. As Guy passed it, he saw a smear of dried blood marred the bent handle. His throat tightened, and he stepped toward the window.

The frame was frozen from long years of neglect, and Guy strained to tug it open. Finally, it rose, showering him with flakes of paint. Blinking dust out of his eyes, Guy leaned through the opening, took Tiff's phone out of his pocket, and held it through the window.

Twenty-four percent battery. No bars. Guy sighed and slumped over the sill. *Maybe I really do need to wait for the rain to clear. Or maybe even that won't be enough. Her phone might never work at Rookward.*

As he made to step away from the window, a single bar flickered into life. Guy froze, staring at it, and fresh hope pumped energy into his veins. But before he could move his thumb to dial a number, the bar vanished again.

"Come on," he said, as if he were speaking to a small child. "Come back. Please."

He extended the phone through the window. As he lifted it higher, the bar flickered back into life. He began dialing. The bar vanished again before he'd entered the third digit.

"Please, please, hang in there for me." He stretched even farther through the window, resting his torso on the frame, and held the phone high. It seemed to do better with altitude, but the bar wouldn't stick. Guy kept trying, stubbornness and desperation making him struggle until well after his rational mind accepted it wasn't going to work. He pulled back inside the room, his arm wet from the spitting rain and the phone devoid of bars.

Anger-infused light flashed across his vision. Guy's fingers tightened around the phone, and the crack on the screen lengthened a millimeter. He forced himself to relax his grip on it then bent over while he waited for the waves of fury to ebb.

The bedroom door behind him drifted open. Guy swiveled, belatedly realizing he hadn't brought a weapon, but the patch of hallway he could see was empty. His lips twisted. *The only way to get higher is to go through the attic. But what if that's what she wants? If I go up there, will I ever come down again?*

Guy ran a hand over his mouth and let his attention shift back to the window. A tendril of the vines poked over the sill and bobbed in the wind. Guy frowned at it then leaned forward, stretching himself over the sill again to see outside. The vines had grown thick on that side of the house, and he hadn't yet attacked their lower supports. One part of the vine in particular caught his eye; it followed a water pipe up the house's wall and clung to the edge of the roof.

"I can make it." Even as he spoke, his stomach tightened. Exhaustion pressed on him, and his leg still ached. But he didn't give caution time to speak. Instead, he moved to the hallway and went in search of the room that shared a wall with the stubborn vines.

CHAPTER 27

GUY CHOSE THE SEWING room. Vines covered half of its window, and the frame had stuck worse than the others. It was so tight that Guy eventually had to resort to bashing it out of its casing with the chair. Shards of glass and wood cascaded down the side of the house, and Guy used his jacket's sleeve to knock the last of them out. Then he flexed his shoulders, felt his pocket to make sure he still had the phone, and crawled through the window.

The chill air bit at him, and specks of rain dotted his skin within seconds. He wriggled around so that his head and shoulders were out of the room but his legs still hung inside. Vines looped all around him, but the patch Guy was especially interested in was to his left. He reached for them, grabbed a fistful, and tugged. The plants were thick and seemed tightly bound to the pipe, and they held better than the ones that clung only to the stones.

A slow footstep scraped down the hallway. Guy peered back into the room just long enough to see a shadow creeping along the hallway's runner. He shuffled himself farther out the window and trusted more weight to the vines and the pipes. Then he stepped out.

For a second, Guy's feet scrambled in the air, then they found purchase on a knotted section of wood. He hugged himself close to the vines and tried not to shake as the water they'd collected soaked into his clothes. Fire radiated from the hurt ankle, but he had no choice except to bear some of his weight on it. The footsteps had reached the room's doorway, but Guy didn't hear them come inside. He took a shallow inhale and began climbing.

Each inch was a battle. Swaths of the vine came away in Guy's hands, but he was reluctant to reach through them and hold the pipe. What patches he could see were badly rusted. The metal made unpleasant clunking noises under his weight, but Guy took advantage of the strange way the vines and pipes were supporting each other. He hugged himself to them as he scaled the wall.

The vines grew thinner the higher he climbed. Guy stopped just below the eaves and balanced himself as well as he could. Then he shifted his weight into his left arm and took his phone out to check the signal.

One bar hovered on the screen long enough for him to dial the number but dropped off before it began to ring. Guy muttered to himself and held the phone out at arm's length as he waited for it to come back. When it did, it stayed for only a second.

"Don't do this to me!" The battery was down to twenty-one

percent. Guy put the phone back in his pocket and eyed the pipe. It ended at the gutter ringing the roof. Parts of the gutter had broken and hung loose, but he thought he might be able to get a hold on it. The roof was sloped but not sharply, and it offered a safer perch than the vine-tangled pipe.

Guy shifted higher then reached an arm over the gutter. The slate roof was slimy from the rain, but when he felt around, he found a hole where one of the tiles had cracked. He tightened his grip on the lip of the hole, took a leap of faith, and released his hold on the pipe entirely.

He dangled for a second, one hand on the gutter and one in the hole in the tiles, straining to pull him up while his feet kicked at the vines and stone wall. The tiles grated together under his hands, threatening to break free. Guy called on his reserves of strength and hauled himself up. Once his torso was over the gutter, he bent forward, using his center of gravity to get onto the roof.

Guy ended up clinging to the tiles, panting and grinning. The drop just a foot away was dizzying, but he tried not to look at it or think about how he would get down. All he cared about was being high enough to get reception. He clambered closer to the roof's peak, using the occasional gaps in the tiles for leverage, then took the phone out once he reached its top.

There was a bar. It didn't disappear. Guy's fingers shook as he dialed his mother's number.

Something moved below him, inside the attic. Guy glanced at the tiles under his feet. He was just above one of the holes in the ceiling, and his foot was propped in it for support. Insulating foam hid the attic from view. He lifted the phone to his ear. It rang once. The scraping sound coming from below was growing closer. Guy shifted back. The opening in the tiles wasn't large enough for a person to fit through, but he still didn't feel comfortable being so close to it.

The phone rang a second time. Guy's fingers shook as he clutched the mobile with both hands. Then there was a click as someone picked up in the middle of the third ring.

A long, pale arm shot out of the ceiling's hole. Guy gasped and tried to jerk away from it. The blood-tinted fingers snatched at his leg and fixed on his shoe.

"Hello?" Heather said.

Guy opened his mouth, either to speak or scream, he wasn't sure. He didn't have the chance to do either. The arm yanked him down the roof, pulling his balance out from under him. His arms pinwheeled as he tried to find purchase, and the damp phone slipped out of his fingers like a bar of soap. He watched it clatter over the tiles, toward the edge of the roof, and disappear over. Then the bloodied hand released him, and he was following the phone, spinning out of control, his fingers being scraped raw as he fought for purchase.

He caught himself on the edge of the roof, his weight bearing down on the gutter. It squealed then jolted him as its bolts came loose. Guy desperately tried to claw his way back onto the tiles. They were too slippery. The gutter collapsed entirely, and he didn't even have time to gasp as he plunged over the edge.

Guy didn't remember hitting the ground. When he opened

his eyes, the sky was above him and a clot of thick vines was below. His vision blurred, and his limbs felt as if they were made of stone, heavy and inflexible. Rain pinged off his face, but he barely felt it. A strange noise wormed its way into his ears. It sounded like sirens.

"Guy?" Dr. Holmes leaned forward in her chair.

Guy startled. He hadn't realized he'd fallen into a daze. "Sorry—"

"It's fine." Her smile was warm. Encouraging. It created tiny crow's feet around her eyes as she nudged her glasses up her long nose and examined her notes. "We're making good progress. So you remember falling off Rookward's roof. Do you recall what happened after that?"

He stared at her, his mind blank. The office was painted in soft, earthy colors, and the wooden bookshelves and ferns created a comforting environment. They weren't helping to soothe the prickling unease in Guy's stomach, though.

"Guy..." She shifted in her leather seat, seeming to choose her words carefully. "Do you remember waking up in hospital? The police interviews? Your mother's death?"

"What?" His chest constricted. He tried to stand, but Dr. Holmes held out a hand to calm him.

"It's all right, Guy. I'm here to help. Take a slow breath. You're going to be fine."

"My mother…" The words caught on his tongue. "She's not—she isn't—"

"You were in a coma for two months. The fall damaged a part of your brain responsible for your memories. It's a form of anterograde amnesia. It's like it's locked you into a point in time. You periodically drift back to that last day at Rookward and lose any memories subsequent to the accident." Dr. Holmes folded her hands over the sheaf of case notes. It was at least an inch thick. "Don't be alarmed. They'll return, slowly."

Guy blinked at the room. It was like seeing it for the first time. But a small voice in the back of his mind insisted the watercolor paintings, tubs of plants, and large bucket chairs were familiar. He swallowed. "I've been here before, haven't I?"

She smiled. "Yes, Guy. Many times. I'm your psychiatrist."

"Why am I seeing you?" He squeezed his hands in his lap. "Is it just because I'm missing memories? I don't have money—"

"It's all right. You don't need to pay for these sessions. They're court mandated."

"Oh." Flashes of memories flitted into Guy's mind. He tried to seize them, but they darted away before he could get a good look. He was afraid to ask the next question. "Why?"

Dr. Holmes hesitated. A deep, horrible dread built in his chest. He couldn't meet her eyes. "What did I do?"

"You killed a girl named Tiffany Price." Dr. Holmes clasped her hands together. Her gaze was sincere, but Guy still couldn't meet it. "The court concluded that you weren't of sound mind when you did it, and you required mental rehabilitation rather than incarceration."

"No." His mouth was hellishly dry. Dr. Holmes had put a glass of water on the small coffee table between them, but he didn't have enough control over his hands to pick it up. "I-I didn't kill her. A tree fell on her. During the storm—"

"Guy, that's a false memory. It's a part of your psychosis. You were under an immense amount of stress when she visited you at Rookward, and when she visited you late one night, you mistook her for one of the phantoms you'd begun to imagine lived around you. She died before you realized what was happening. So you carried her outside, placed her next to a fallen tree, and your mind built a complex series of events to explain her death."

Guy stared. His pulse rushed in his ears, and his world became very small. "No. Please, that's not what happened. I didn't hurt her! I wouldn't— "

But the memories were bubbling up like toxic ichor from the bottom of a lake. Guy saw himself bringing down his crowbar again and again, fear and frantic anger taking hold of his limbs until the girl's head was a pulp of crushed bones and gore.

He dug his fingers into his hair, pulling hard enough to hurt, as a horrified, miserable wail rose inside of him. He'd thrown away her car keys. He'd written the note that he would later discover tucked into her pocket. He'd faked her death.

"It's all right, Guy. Take a breath. Ground yourself." Dr. Holmes waited until Guy lowered his shaking fingers.

He felt hopelessly, helplessly lost. Dr. Holmes leaned close, scanning his features, and eventually continued in a softer voice. "You can't blame yourself for what happened to Tiffany Price. You never intended to hurt anyone. This is something we've been working on—learning how to forgive yourself for your past. Not just Miss Price's death, but also Savannah's."

Guy snapped his head up to meet Dr. Holmes's dark eyes. Dread churned in his stomach. "Please, I can't have hurt Savannah—"

She continued in a softer voice. "Your psychosis began on the day you hit Savannah, killing her and her unborn child. The grief and horror were too great for you to cope with, so your mind constructed an alternative world—one where Savannah and her child lived but simply didn't want to see you again. I'm not telling you this to hurt you, Guy. I'm here to help. And the first steps to recovery are facing your reality, no matter how painful."

"No." Guy tried to squeeze his eyes shut against the memory, but nothing could keep it out. As Dr. Holmes's words washed over him, he heard the thud then the crunch as the pickup truck hit Savannah. He remembered leaping out, screaming in terror and horror, and trying to pull her free. There was so much blood…

"You're going to be all right, Guy." Dr. Holmes pulled her chair closer to his. Her eyes traced over his face, and her lips tightened in concern. "I'll be here to help you. For as long as you need."

Guy dropped his head into his hands. Desperate, plaintive sobs wrenched their way out of his chest. He almost wished he were back at Rookward, trapped in the fantasy he'd built; at least there, he wasn't a murderer. At least there, Savannah and his baby daughter were still alive, even if he never saw them. His mother was waiting for him to come home. He had hope. A future.

"I don't want to live like this," he whispered. "Not when I've lost everything."

"It feels that way right now, but it's not the truth." She bent closer. "You can survive this. You're strong; you can go on to have a happy, satisfying life. You may even find love again."

Dr. Holmes's hand rested on his knee. The long fingers rubbed at his jeans. He glanced up.

She was familiar—even more familiar than the office. Her dark eyes and high cheekbones reminded him of someone. He was sure...

"This isn't right." Guy stood. Dizziness washed through him. The office was distorting in tiny ways. The potted vines were identical, like photocopies. He stumbled toward the nearest bookcase, but none of the volumes had any titles on their spines.

"You need to calm down, Thomas." Dr. Holmes folded her hands over her long legs. The psychiatrist Guy had visited for his anger wore loose pants and a simple, modest top and jacket. But Dr. Holmes was dressed in a skirt and had her dark hair up in a style that appeared more suited to the sixties.

"This isn't real," Guy said, and the room dissolved. The house-plants morphed into dark, twisted vines. The coffee table became the old black-and-white TV, its screen still smashed from when he'd thrown it out the window. And the bucket chair he'd been lounging in was the bloodstained couch.

Guy stepped back. He was in Rookward's family room, and Amy was nowhere to be seen.

CHAPTER 28

GUY CHOKED ON HIS hysterical cry. He doubled over, his hands gripping his hair, as his mind spun.

How did I get here? Did she move me while I was unconscious? He turned toward the window. Tiff's car was barely visible near the edge of the forest, where early-afternoon light glinted off the metal. *She wanted me to think I was insane. Why? So that I would trust her?*

It had worked, Guy was ashamed to admit. For the brief moments he'd spoken with Amy, he'd believed her every word. She hadn't just distorted his vision, but planted conviction in his mind, as well. She'd made him relive the day he'd hit Savannah… except in her twisted reality, blood had splattered across the scene. The horror clenched his stomach.

But Savannah isn't dead. I remember staring at her across the courtroom and bumping into her that day at the library. But for that moment, Amy made me really believe I'd killed her.

And Tiff, too. She convinced me I was to blame. He pictured the phantom memory again—the crowbar rising and falling, spraying up chunks of bone—and retched. He leaned against the wall, shaking and clammy.

She tried to take everything from me—not just Savannah, but also my mother, my freedom, and my sanity. If I hadn't recognized her, how long would she have kept me there? Days? Months? The rest of my life?

The illusion hadn't been perfect, though. She had created a bookcase but didn't know any titles to put on it. The plants were imperfect. None of the room's details had been very clear, even when he'd looked at them closely. And she'd only known how to dress from the era when she'd been alive.

He rubbed at his goose-bumped arms. The illusion had felt real enough to bring tears to his eyes. He started to go back to the dining room, and that was when he became aware of the pain.

His leg—the same leg with the cuts—now ached right up to the hipbone. When he pressed on it, the flesh was sensitive. Guy limped to the dining room and pulled a small mirror out of the pack of toiletries. It was too small to show more than flashes of his person, but what it revealed wasn't great. Blood was smeared from his hairline and ran down one cheek. Leaves and fragments of organic matter had collected in his hair. And bruises were already starting to form on his cheek, arm, and undoubtedly his leg.

It could be worse. Guy put away the mirror. That fall could have killed him. He was probably alive thanks to those hellish vines he'd landed on.

Sighing, he let his head dip, then a thought occurred to him. He patted his pockets, but of course, the phone wasn't in them. It had tumbled over the roof's edge before he fell.

"Damn, damn, damn." He hopped through the house's back door. The drizzling rain hadn't abated, but he was already so wet that it didn't make much of a difference. Guy moved around the house's outside as quickly as his leg would let him, then he stopped under the part of the roof he'd fallen from. The gutter dangled above him. One side was still attached, and the metal squealed as the wind made it swing. Guy fell to his knees and began scrambling through the flattened vegetation where he'd landed.

"C'mon, where are you?" Thorns pricked his fingers, but he ignored them as he dug loose clumps of the vine away and shook them out.

A metallic glint caught his eye. Guy gasped and grabbed for it. He lifted the precious phone to examine it in the light.

The crack on the screen had extended across the entire face, and it was dripping water. Guy pressed the power button, then his heart plunged when it didn't respond.

Did I crush it? Did it run out of power? Or did the water kill it?

Unable to stand giving up on his only hope of contacting the outside world, he clutched the phone close to his chest as he hopped back into the kitchen. He found a bag of rice he'd brought in one of the crates, tore it open with his teeth, and poured it into a saucepan. He buried the phone inside. If rain was responsible for killing the phone, the rice would absorb some of it…he hoped.

Guy rubbed water off the tip of his nose. Sickening exhaustion combined with the multitude of aches to make him wish he could just curl into a ball on the ground and give up. He thought of his mother. He pictured what his death would do to her, imagined her having to arrange his funeral and stand at the graveside alone. No one from the town would rally around her to bury the man they despised. He was all she had, in the same way she was all he had.

A new idea occurred to him, and it made Guy's limbs turn cold. Heather had answered the phone just as Amy attacked. She wouldn't have recognized Tiff's number and might assume it was a prank call. But she was also a worrier and had been anxious about Guy's stay at Rookward—with good cause, as it turned out. *How much of the struggle did she hear? Would a call from a foreign number be enough to alarm her? Is there any chance she would drive out here to check on me?*

Fear made his palms clammy. Amy seemed obsessed with removing other women from Guy's life, and Tiff's death had been violent and merciless. He didn't want to imagine what the specter would do to Heather if she tried to enter Rookward's grounds.

I need to get back to her. Guy rolled his shoulders and tried to ignore the pain. *There's got to be a way out of here. Something I haven't thought of yet.*

He moved to the window and stared at where the driveway disappeared into the trees. He could try walking out again, but he knew the chance that it would turn out better than the last time was laughably small. In fact, he suspected it would turn out much worse; he didn't think he had the energy to walk for an entire day again.

Finding Tiff's keys would be like looking for a needle in a haystack, except he didn't know where the haystack was. And if he found them, there was always the risk Amy had sabotaged the car just like she had with his. He could hope the phone could be revived, but he couldn't afford to put his trust in it.

His truck was worth another try. He still didn't know what was wrong with it, but if he could find the problem, it might be possible to raid Tiff's car for parts.

Amy's what's wrong with it. Guy snorted and rubbed at the corners of his eyes. He didn't have high hopes for saving his beloved pickup.

But there wasn't any other way to escape Rookward. Unless… Guy's head snapped up. While hiking through the forest, he'd passed a river shortly before arriving back at the house. He could construct a raft and escape along it.

Amy might be able to distort what he could see. She could turn him around in the forest, lead him back home, and even convince his mind he was in a therapist's office. But there wasn't much she could do to a river. Once Guy was on it, the current could only carry him one direction—away from Rookward.

Hope gave him energy. He yanked open the crate of depleted supplies. He'd used all of the duct tape on the upstairs attic blockade, but he still had string, nails, and screws. He collected them into a crate, along with hammers and saws, and dragged them outside. The clouds obscured most of the sun, but he guessed the day was progressing toward late afternoon. He still had some hours of daylight left.

Chills had set in to Guy's limbs. He clenched his teeth and squinted against the rain as he turned toward the patch of forest he thought led to the water.

It wasn't a long walk. The ground began to slope downhill, then Guy picked up on the telltale rushing, bubbling noises. He stepped out from behind a curtain of lichen and found himself on the river's shore, not far from the trunk he'd crawled along to reach Rookward.

Guy dropped his supplies and scanned the area. There was plenty of wood to build a raft. The only thing he was missing was know-how. Before coming to Rookward, he'd watched a plethora of tutorial videos for sealing floors, painting, repairing broken windows, and patching roofs, but he'd never considered he might need to construct an emergency escape raft.

It doesn't have to sail across the ocean. Guy took the saw out and began cutting branches off a nearby tree. *It just has to get me far enough away from Rookward that Amy can't follow.*

That posed another question: how far could she travel? He was certain she'd stalked him through the woods. *Is it possible she's latched on to me, rather than the house, and I'll never be free from her?*

It was a chilling thought, but Guy tried to dismiss it. Dwelling on future possibilities wouldn't help; he just had to focus on his immediate task and deal with whatever came next when it arrived.

The job wasn't quick. Finding straight sticks of equal width was nearly impossible, and Guy's numb fingers were soon coated with sap and tiny nicks as he stripped the leaves off and tried to screw the lengths together. He chose a very basic raft shape—twelve branches the width of his arm strapped together to create a flat platform. It wouldn't protect him much from either the weather or the river, but when he tested it by applying pressure, the raft seemed sturdy enough, and he was confident it would float.

Guy made a final trip back to Rookward to collect supplies. He took the bag he'd left outside the kitchen door—it still held two cans of soup—and re-filled the water jug from the tarp in the back of the pickup truck. As he strode away from the building, he threw a glance over his shoulder. A tall, thin figure pressed against one of the second-floor windows. Guy couldn't see her features, but he could feel the intensity of her gaze on him. He hitched the bag up his shoulder and pushed his exhausted body to limp to his escape point.

The river was swollen and running quickly thanks to the deluge of rain. Guy fashioned himself a pole from a long, thin sapling then tied his bag of supplies to the center of the raft. He pushed the structure halfway into the river then crept onto it. The water dragged at the wood, making it shake and lurch before it was even afloat, and Guy felt a twinge of misgiving.

He couldn't see more than twenty meters ahead before the river twisted out of sight. Trees hung low over the rushing water, and Guy knew he was running the risk of hitting another trunk fallen over the stream. If he got tipped out of the raft before reaching any kind of civilization, he could very well freeze overnight.

But it was better than returning to Rookward. Guy crouched low in the center of his raft and used the stick to push away from shore.

The river snatched the small craft up easily. Water rushed through the gaps between the logs, frothing around Guy's legs, but it was buoyant and large enough that it didn't immediately overturn. Guy kept his center of gravity low and clung to the stumps of the small branches he'd sawn off. The raft picked up speed alarmingly quickly, and Guy soon had to release his hold so that he could use the stick to keep the craft from becoming jammed in patches of weeds or on either of the riverbanks.

The plan was working, though. A spike of adrenaline made Guy hysterical with excitement, and a wild laugh burst out of him, startling a flock of dark birds out of a nearby tree. The icy rain hitting his face and the rough wood digging into his sore leg couldn't compare with the thrill of being rushed downstream.

There's nothing she can do now. A rock jutted out of the water ahead, and Guy shoved his pole into it to keep the raft clear. He skated around and kept moving. *She can't reverse the river's flow. She can't confuse me or turn me back toward Rookward.*

The slope took a sharp dip, and Guy yelped as he was caught in rapids. He tried to guide the raft around the rocks, but an impact jarred his arm so badly that the pole was torn out of his grip. He tried to snatch it out of the frothing water, but he had to flatten himself against the splintery wood to keep from being tipped over the side.

Guy swore and clung to his craft with all of his strength. Water rushed into his mouth. He hit a rock, then another, bouncing off them like a bumper car. A cracking noise warned him the craft had taken damage. Then the frothing water calmed again, and Guy felt brave enough to lift his head.

Water ran out of his hair, plastering it to his forehead and getting into his eyes, and he wiped them clear. The river had widened to at least forty feet across, and the flow had slowed. Thick reeds poked out of both shores, and humming insects flitted through them. Without his pole, Guy had no way to direct the craft. The log farthest to his left had taken a hit hard enough to wrench its screw out, and it bobbed loose from the rest of the craft, only attached by two nails near the end. It was a hazard, so Guy kicked it loose to unburden the raft.

The trees lining the bloated river seemed different from the ones that grew around Rookward. They were straighter and held more leaves, and some of them grew flowers. The change was subtle, but after staring at the gnarled, darkened plants around Rookward for so many days, Guy was grateful for the fresh sight. He didn't know where the river led, but that was a trivial detail as long as he eventually reached some kind of habitation.

He sat back on the raft, moving carefully to avoid unbalancing it, and took a deep inhale. Even the air tasted fresher and cleaner. Only one small thing existed to remind him of the house; a soft scratching noise, so much like the scrabbling he'd heard in the attic.

Guy looked down. Something was clinging to the underside of his raft. Something dark and large—

A round, urgent eye peered up at him through one of the gaps between the logs. Guy jerked back, a scream tearing out of him. Long fingers stretched through the hole, wriggling horribly as they tried to grasp at his legs. There was nowhere for Guy to escape to. His breath caught as he tried to stomp on the fingers, to detach the woman who'd latched on to his raft.

He hit a rock. He hadn't seen it coming; even if he had, there would have been no way to avoid it. But leaned back as he was, the impact was enough to destabilize the raft.

Guy felt it turning and threw himself forward, toward the scrabbling fingers. He was too late. The raft flipped, and Guy experienced a second of weightlessness as he was tossed into the air. Then freezing-cold water enveloped him.

The river snatched him into its embrace, tumbling him and twirling him like a leaf in the wind. He couldn't fight the impulse to gasp. Water flooded his lungs. He thrashed, fighting to reach the surface, but something cold and slimy slid around his body.

Amy threaded her arms around his torso. Legs tangled with his. She pulled him down, sinking them both with the intimate embrace. Bubbles escaped Guy's mouth as he scrabbled at the arm locked around his throat. He felt her kiss his cheek, her lips somehow even colder than the water.

Guy's lungs were on fire. He hit a rock, but the impact barely hurt. Blackness swallowed his vision until even the distant sparkles of light bouncing off the river's surface vanished. Then it was just him and Amy, coiled together in the dark.

CHAPTER 29

"SWEETIE?" SOMEONE SHOOK HIS shoulders. "Sweetie, can you hear me?"

Guy coughed. A mouthful of lukewarm water poured over his chin. He rolled onto his side, gasping air into his starved lungs. His head throbbed. His vision was blurry. But somehow, he was alive.

"You're gonna be fine, honey." A woman pressed a cloth to his forehead.

Guy blinked up at her. She was dressed in simple flannels and had her long hair knotted at the base of her neck. Her smile was kind, if a little weary, and creases aged her face. He squinted past her to see his surroundings.

He was in some kind of farmhouse. The space had been decorated with woods and furs, and paintings of flowers hung on the walls. A lit fireplace was at his back, and the heat radiating off the flames felt good on his frozen limbs. Someone had draped a blanket over his lower half, and a plush rug cushioned his aching limbs.

Despite the comfort surrounding him, vague concern gnawed at the inside of Guy's chest. He felt as though he should be worried about something—he just couldn't remember what. When he spoke, his throat felt raw. "Where am I?"

"Safe, honey." The woman's smile widened a fraction. She didn't seem threatening; she was plump and sweet and drawled her words. "I found you on the riverbank. Thought you were dead at first. But you pulled through, eh?"

She turned toward the couch behind her, and Guy realized an older man and two children sat there. The man gave him a curt nod while the children dozed at his side.

"Thank you." Guy tried to sit up, but dizziness made his head pound. He couldn't shake the feeling that something was wrong, but every time he reached for the source of the anxiety, it danced away.

The woman pushed him back down with soft hands. "Don't you worry about anything, sweetie. Rest for a bit. I'll make you some soup, all right?"

Soup sounded amazing, but Guy still couldn't relax. He blinked against the white dots floating across his vision. "Uh, can I make a call, please?"

"Ooh." The woman's smile drooped. "I'm sorry, the storms knocked our phone lines out. We're gonna be stuck here for a couple of days. But it's okay, this house is safe from the flood-waters, and you're welcome to stay with us until the road clears."

Guy nodded and settled back onto his makeshift bed. His mind felt foggy, as if the previous days had been just a vivid, exceptionally unsettling dream.

The woman rose and folded her towel as she moved into the kitchen. The man on the couch gazed at the crackling fireplace, his expression serene as he brushed the hair away from his sleeping son's forehead.

"Thanks for letting me stay," Guy said, and the farmer gave him a short, unsmiling nod.

The room was peaceful and warm, and his hosts were welcoming. Still, the scene didn't feel quite right. The man on the couch reminded Guy of someone. It took him a minute to realize who, but when he did, he bolted upright. He'd seen the farmer before, many times, in his dreams.

Guy twisted to stare at the woman in the kitchen. She'd disguised her face and her voice, but her long, dark hair was unmistakable. Sickening dread flooded through Guy to wash out any sense of comfort the setting had instilled in him.

Not again. Please, not again. I don't want to go back there.

"Something wrong, honey?" The farmer's wife shot him a smile over her shoulder. She'd found a way to soften her cheekbones and make her irises a light hazel, but there was too much of Amy in her bearing and the long, pale fingers that chopped a carrot.

"You're not real," Guy said, and the illusion began to disintegrate. The family on the couch—Thomas, Daniel, and Rebecca—went first. Like a clump of cotton candy dropped into water, they bled away, desaturating then evaporating. The fire went out, leaving Guy cold and sore. Then the plush rug morphed into the guest room's thin carpet. Guy blinked, and the warm, happy farmhouse was gone.

He would have cried if he could have found the energy to. It was a special kind of cruelty to offer him everything he wanted then snatch it away again. He stared at his hands, bruised, scratched, and aching, then looked up.

He was in the guest room. Amy had placed him beside the dead fireplace below the clock. The couches had returned to the room, even though he'd dismantled them and thrown them out. Apparently, the specter didn't like it when he changed the house.

Amy stood in the doorway, watching him. She was very different from the severe but beautiful woman he'd seen in Thomas's memories. Her skin held no color, and her dark hair hung limp around her face and cascaded over the shoulders of her gray slip dress. A sheen of white covered her pupils, and although she stared at Guy, he had the impression she was looking through him, not at him.

"Leave me alone!" Guy snatched the ornate clock off the fire's mantelpiece and hurled it at the specter. She faded from sight as it passed through the place where her head had been. Guy, breathing heavily, waited for her to return. When she didn't, he pressed his hands over his face as his shoulders shook.

More illusions. How can she twist my reality so thoroughly?

He dropped his hands and faced the window. The sun was close to setting; the treetops' silhouettes stood out in stark contrast against the sky. He didn't know if Amy had somehow teleported him back to the house or whether she'd made him walk back while his mind wasn't conscious, but his legs ached enough for the latter. The thought of spending another night at Rookward was unbearable.

He could see the fallen tree and Tiff's car but no sign of his mother's sedan. That was a relief but not a reprieve. Guy had no way of knowing how much the call might have unnerved his mother, but the longer he was gone, the more she was likely to worry, until it finally culminated in some kind of action. It could still be days before she came looking for him, but eventually, she would—and the only way to keep her safe would be to escape the property first.

But how can I leave when Amy distorts reality? I'm living in a world controlled by her rules. Anything I see and hear might be filtered through her lies.

A thought flashed into Guy's consciousness. His eyes widened. It sounded too good to be true, but he couldn't stop the small seed of hope from growing.

He pushed exhausted limbs to carry him through the guest room's doorway. A shudder wracked him as he passed the place Amy had stood. He couldn't see her, but he could feel her watching him as he continued outside.

The pickup truck waited for him with the keys in its ignition. Guy wrenched open the door and slid inside. His limbs ached as he bent them to fit, but the soft seat felt good. He turned the key, and the car made the familiar clicking noise. Guy bit his lip and put the car in gear, released the hand break, and put his foot on the accelerator.

He lurched forward, and a huge, shocked grin lit his face. *Another illusion. She masked the engine's noise to make me think it was broken, but my pickup is fine.*

Hysterical laughter broke out of him. He couldn't believe it—his escape had been just outside the door, waiting for him the whole time. The lack of motor noises was disquieting, but it didn't stop the wheels from turning as he guided the truck toward the driveway's edge. The tarp full of water sloshed, spilling over the truck bed to pour across the long weeds, but Guy didn't want to stop long enough to empty it.

He sped up as he neared the driveway's start. His heart thundered, and he squeezed the wheel, coaxing his vehicle to gain speed as it careened toward his escape.

The truck came to a sharp, harsh halt. The sound of crunching metal filled the space, and Guy was thrown forward into the deployed airbag. Pain burst through his head as pressure built in his already-bruised skull. He snapped back into the seat, gasping, and blinked as the airbag began to deflate.

He'd driven off the road and hit a tree.

CHAPTER 30

THE TREE WASN'T LARGE, but it had been solid enough to crumple the truck's hood. A plume of black smoke spiraled out of the engine.

"No." *How did I not see it? I was following the driveway...* He put the car in reverse and tried to back away from the obstacle. The pickup wouldn't budge. "No, please...come on, no!"

Guy threw open the door and jumped out. The impact had dug the tree halfway out of the ground and created a massive fissure in its trunk. Fresh sap was already beading around the impact. The truck was in worse shape; its hood rippled like an accordion, and dark oil dripped onto the ground below.

Another illusion. Instead of building fantasies, though, she'd stopped him from seeing something that really existed. Boiling anger surged up inside him. Guy clutched at his head, trying to hold it inside, but it felt as though it were shredding his organs.

He screamed and kicked at the tree, then beat it, punching the wood until his knuckles were scraped raw and aching. The hatred tasted like black tar filling his mouth. His vision went dark. Guy reeled back, fingers twitching, and a roaring sound filled his ears. As the fury waned, he spat a swear word and began pacing. He thumped his fist against the fractured tree every time he passed it.

She'll never let me leave. No matter what I try, she's prepared for it and knows exactly how to foil it. I have no more hope of escaping than Thomas did.

He ran his hands over his face. The building watched over him, calm and infinitely patient. He loathed it and its twisted occupant. But in a strange way, he no longer feared it. Sometime within the last day, without even realizing it, he'd come to accept he would likely die at Rookward. He still fought for survival, but it was from principle, not hope. The building was designed to be his tomb.

No more running. No more hiding.

Guy took his time returning to the building. Daylight was almost gone, and he wanted to savor its final moments. He ran the tips of his fingers through the long weeds, flicking insects and droplets of rain off them, before facing the black hole that marked the kitchen door.

He could hear Amy pacing upstairs as he reentered the building. Her footsteps scraped over the runner in a corpse's shuffle. He was ready to climb the stairs and face her, but first, he stopped in the dining room to pull Tiff's phone out of the bowl of rice.

He pressed the power button. To his surprise, it came on. He waited for the logo to fade and be replaced with the home screen. No bars. Four percent battery. He turned it back off and tucked it into his pocket.

Confronting Amy felt like a moment of no return. He would either find a way to shake free of her or be sucked so far into the mire that he would never surface. The thought of never leaving Rookward hit him hard enough to make his knees buckle, and he braced himself against the table.

Never leaving Rookward means never seeing Mum again. Never having another chance to glimpse Savannah. Never even knowing my daughter's name.

He reached for the notepad he'd used for measurements and tore off three clean sheets.

At the top of the first note, Guy wrote HEATHER. He kept the message short but heartfelt. He thanked her for always believing in him and loving him. He told her she was the best mother he could have hoped for, and that she'd made his life good. Finally, he asked her not to hold any guilt for what had happened to him. It had been his choice to come to Rookward, and she couldn't have done anything to change the outcome. He finished it with the salutation, "Love you forever, Guy" and underlined the phrase twice.

He addressed the second note to Savannah. It was harder to write, and he sat for minutes at a time, trying to find the right way to phrase his feelings. The scrape of footsteps never ceased, adding to Guy's stress and making his hand shake as he formed the words. The final version felt clumsy and embarrassingly intimate, but every word was honest.

Savannah,

I wish I could find the words to express the depth of my regret. I never wanted to hurt you, but I did, and I hate myself for the pain I put you through. You didn't deserve the accident or my temper. I'm so sorry.

I hope you find a good man, one who will cherish you and protect you like I should have. I won't ask for your forgiveness, but instead, I hope any memories you have of me don't hurt you. I want you to be happy.

I have one request. Please don't tell our daughter I was violent. If she ever asks about me, tell her I adored her and wanted to be her father. Say she made me happy, that I loved her, and that I wish I could have been with her as she grew up.

All of my love to both you and your daughter.

Guy

He wiped at the cool tracks of dampness running down his cheek then set the two sheets on top of each other at the head of the table. The final message only took a moment to write, and it went on top of the other pages, where it would be seen first.

This house is dangerous. Leave immediately. You're not safe as long as you're in it.

If, by some miracle, he survived, he could tear up the papers before leaving. But that was a very ominous *if.* Guy let his shoulders slump. The notes were the best he could do for the people he cherished, and he hoped they would be enough.

The scraping footsteps persisted as Amy traversed the upstairs hall like a pacing tiger. Guy scratched his fingers through his hair then stood, squared his shoulders, and moved toward the stairs.

The upstairs hallway was nearly perfectly lightless. Guy fixed his gaze on the landing as he climbed the steps, one hand running along the dust-shrouded banister. A shadow flitted across the dark ceiling. Guy licked his chapped, blood-tinged lips.

"Amy?" He came to a stop on the landing and glanced to either side. The master bedroom's door shifted open, drawing inward in a smooth, slow arc. Guy hesitated for only a second before stepping inside.

If she wanted to kill me, she's had a multitude of opportunities. Guy squeezed his hands at his sides and straightened his spine. *It might still be possible to reason with her.*

"Amy? I want to talk." He scanned the room's shadows. The space was too dim, and Guy regretted not bringing the lamp with him. "Can you hear me?"

Something icy ran across the back of Guy's neck. He sucked in a startled gasp. He could feel her behind him, hovering just an inch away, but he didn't want to turn. If he turned, he would have to confront those awful, glassy, staring eyes.

Her words were so soft that Guy could barely hear them. "I've been waiting for you."

"I know." He swallowed, squeezing his shaking hands together to hide the tremors. "I want to go home."

"*This* is your home, Thomas." She laughed.

The sound made Guy's stomach clench. "I'm not Thomas, and this isn't my house." He tilted his head to catch a glimpse of her bloodless lips smiling from behind his shoulder. "I want to leave."

"Don't be silly, my darling. You can't leave. Not ever. You promised you'd stay with me." Long fingers topped with harsh nails dug into Guy's arms. She kissed the nape of his neck. "I'll make you happy."

A shudder ran through Guy in response to her touch. He twisted just far enough to see her features. "I told you I'm not Thomas. My name is Guy. You killed the real Thomas fifty years ago. Don't you remember?"

Amy's face twitched. Her eyes darkened, and her nails pierced his skin. Then she blinked. The smile was back in place, but it felt tenuous, dangerous. Anger flickered under the surface. "Darling, you're not making any sense. I've been excessively patient. Why do you insist on playing these games?"

Guy hated seeing the bloodless, distorted face, but he refused to let himself look away. He felt like he was walking a razor's edge. Saying he wasn't Thomas made her furious. He didn't think her temper would hold if he followed that line of argument any further, and even if he could break through the delusions and convince Amy that her lover was gone, he doubted he would be allowed to leave the house alive. He tried a different tactic. "What do you want from me?"

"Your devotion." The kisses moved up his throat, then her teeth nipped the sensitive skin just under his chin.

Guy locked his muscles into place to stop himself from flinching away. "In what way?"

"I was willing to die for you. Will you do the same for me, Thomas?"

"You want me dead?"

"Yes." The delight was clear in her voice. She pressed her body against his back. It didn't feel fully solid and was horrifically cold. Something sharp prodded at his side, just below his ribs. *A knife?* "We can be together then. Forever."

Why wasn't the real Thomas trapped here after his death? Is it because she killed him, instead of him choosing to die? Shivers wracked through Guy. He wet his parched lips. The words were almost impossible to say, but he forced them out and added as much conviction as he was capable of. "All right, I'll stay with you. But I want something first. My mother will miss me; let me call her to say goodbye."

Amy's fingers squeezed his arms a fraction tighter, burning the flesh, then she stepped back. Both her touch and the icy chill she brought abated.

Guy turned. The hallway was empty. He closed his eyes and placed his hand over his heart, which galloped painfully. He wanted to drop to the floor and give his body a chance to recover, but he had no time. The phone's battery was nearly dead.

He followed the hall toward the trapdoor. The house stayed mercifully silent. Only Guy's ragged breathing disturbed the stillness. He stopped under his duct-taped tripod blocking the trapdoor. That was one thing he hadn't planned for—he had no way to cut the structure apart. But as he stared at it, the tape shriveled up, falling off the boards like magic.

Guy stepped back as the structure collapsed. As the third board clattered against the wall, the trapdoor fell open, and the retractable ladder tumbled down to clatter against the carpet. Guy glanced behind himself, but he was alone. He rubbed at the raised hairs over his arms then stepped onto the ladder and began climbing.

CHAPTER 31

THE ATTIC FELT DISCONNECTED from the downstairs room. Stepping into it was like stepping into another world—and it was a dark, twisted one. Guy tried not to stare at the shadows coiling along the walls and ceiling. It was impossible to tell whether Amy was in the space with him, hunched behind the cluster of crates she'd made her home, perhaps, or if he'd grown so paranoid that he was imagining her everywhere he went.

Guy took the phone out of his pocket. Two percent battery. One bar. He held the mobile like a drowning man clutching a fragment of wood. Fear thudded through his veins. After this call, he would be out of options. It was a Hail Mary before he was at Amy's mercy.

He dialed the emergency number.

It was answered almost immediately. Before the person on

the other end could speak, Guy snapped, his words rushed and urgent, "189 Greenhaven Street, Faulconbridge. I need he—"

Burning-hot pain pierced the center of his back. Guy's hands spasmed, and he dropped the phone. It clattered to the floor. The screen remained lit for another second, then it went black as the battery finally failed.

Guy gasped and took a staggering pace forward. Amy stood behind him, her expression contorted, a red-coated kitchen knife clutched in her hands.

"Liar!" she shrieked. Saliva flew from her mouth, and a vein bulged in her colorless neck. "Liar, cheater, traitor!"

Guy raised his hand against the blow, but he couldn't stop it. She plunged the knife into his stomach. He doubled over, but only a thin whine of pain escaped his throat. Amy drew the knife back out and thrust it home a third time.

She clutched him close, and her freezing breath ghosted over his neck. "Why do you torment me like this, Thomas? Why do you make me fight so hard for you?"

"No—" Guy's legs gave out.

Amy fell to the ground with him, her arms tangled around his torso like a lover. A loud rushing noise filled his ears. He blinked, but he couldn't see. He tried to move—to push the specter away from him—but his limbs only twitched.

Amy's expression shifted from fury to gentle concern. "Shh, be calm now, my dear. We can be together still. I'll take care of you."

She twisted the knife. Guy's vision went black.

He stood in Rookward's library. The shelves and chairs were familiar but wholly different from the view he'd become used to. The bookcases were overflowing with untitled volumes of all sizes, and the furniture had been returned to its original state: clean, attractive, and impeccably matched to the room's décor.

Two children stood in one of the doorways. They were dressed in what Guy's mother would have called their Sunday best. The girl's hair was tied back into bunches at the back of her neck, and the boy's shoes glinted in the golden light. But their faces were empty. Neither had eyes nor a mouth, only gentle slopes and ridges to indicate the spaces where the features belonged. Guy recoiled and bumped into one of the chairs. The children neither moved nor spoke, but stood straight as a pin.

The door leading to the foyer opened, and Guy felt his heart skip a beat. Amy stood in the entryway. The pale-skinned, glassy-eyed specter that had tormented him was gone. Her dark hair cascaded around her shoulders, and her ruby-red lips curled up, drawing attention to her high cheekbones and sparkling eyes.

She swirled a magnificent red dress around herself as she strolled toward Guy. "Hello, darling."

He swallowed. The eyeless children continued to stare. He nodded in their direction and forced his voice to work. "Did you do that?"

"I made them for you, my dear." She tilted her head to the side, sending her diamond earrings bouncing. "They're the perfect children, aren't they? They don't speak, and they don't judge. They're there when you want them and never when you don't."

It's sick. You're sick. Guy swallowed the words. He backed away from Amy as far as he could, but she cornered him against one of the bookcases.

She lifted a hand and caressed Guy's cheek. Her flesh was warm, but the rings on her fingers were chilled. He shivered.

"This is the way it was always supposed to be," she whispered.

Guy's stomach clenched as she ran the hand from his cheek down over his chest. He was wearing a suit, he realized. It was crisp and dry, unlike the clothes he'd been wearing in the attic.

Amy played with the buttons as she smiled up at him. "You and me. Delighting in each other's company. Forever."

I'd prefer death. Again, Guy swallowed the words. Infuriating the woman wouldn't help. He needed to keep his mind clear, but it was hard when she kept shifting closer to him.

"I've longed to dance with you, my darling." As the words left her mouth, music filled the room. Guy recognized a waltz. Amy nodded to the children, and like machines, they strode out of the room. She placed one hand on Guy's shoulder and tugged his arm around her waist.

Guy's stomach revolted against the touch, but an idea had occurred to him, and he battled the impulse to pull away. Instead, he put his arm around her waist, squared his shoulders, and led Amy into the dance.

He hadn't waltzed since his prom, when he and Savannah had

been a couple. He remembered the way she'd rested her head against his shoulder. He'd never felt so warm or giddy before. He latched on to the memory, one of the few that hadn't been tainted by his temper or the accident, and twirled Amy through the room.

She closed her eyes in delight as they danced. They kept the pace brisk and smooth. Guy swirled her out of the library and into the hallway. Dozens of pictures hung on the walls. They showed Guy and Amy together, embracing and, in some cases, kissing. Guy looked happy in the pictures. He forced his lips to mimic the smile as Amy sighed against his shoulder.

"I knew it would all be worth it," she murmured.

Guy led her into the dining room. The table had been cleaned and set with lit candelabras and two settings of fine china. He danced with Amy around the table and into the kitchen. A roast in the oven smelled so good that saliva flooded Guy's mouth. He spun her in a little twirl in the center of the room then pulled her close. She pressed one hand against his chest and leaned her head on his shoulder. She didn't seem to notice how plastic his smile was.

"I knew, as soon as I met you, we were meant to be together." She rubbed her cheek against his neck. "It was all worth it. Leaving home, hiding in your attic while we waited for a chance to be rid of your wife—even when you left me, I knew you weren't really gone. You would find your way back to me."

Guy took his hand off her hip to run it through her black hair. Touching her made his skin crawl, but he stroked her slowly, how he had once stroked Savannah. Their earlier tempo had fallen to a slow step. He'd angled their bodies so that his back was to the kitchen counter. When he took his hand off her hair, he reached behind himself. Her eyes were closed. She didn't notice as his fingers fixed around the knife left on the empty cutting board.

This is for Tiff. He tightened his hand around the cold metal. *For Thomas, Louise, and their children. For forcing my mother to bury her child. For every life you've ruined. Rot in hell.*

He thrust the knife into her back. Her eyes popped open and met Guy's. Shock marred her face as he withdrew the knife, then she stumbled back. He followed her retreat, bringing the blade into her throat, her torso, her abdomen—any place he could reach. The anger he'd been keeping in check reared up, sending fire through his limbs and turning his vision black, and he embraced it.

He'd never intentionally hurt a human before. That was a line he'd drawn and never crossed, no matter how bad the fury—but he crossed it then, willingly and recklessly. The knife cut through her ribs, her abdomen, and her collarbone. He hacked at any part of her he could reach.

The fury turned his vision black, then red, and he tumbled on top of her, his own pulse deafening, the need to cut into the creature below him overwhelming. He didn't try to moderate the anger but let it lend him strength as it roared through him like a hurricane. He felt bones break. Blood soaked his arms and splattered across his bared teeth, but he was senseless to the taste.

The knife's blade broke off. He tossed it aside and used his fists instead to pulp the fragile bones in the monster's face.

Stop. The little voice in the back of his mind spoke so softly that he barely heard it. *Stop, Guy, before you go too far to come back.*

His fingers dug into gore and flung clumps of it aside. It felt good—cathartic—like taking a deep gasp after being starved of oxygen.

Stop, Guy, this isn't you. This isn't the man you want to be.

Wild laughter tore out of him. Specks of light danced across his red-tinted vision. The crackle of cartilage was beautiful; he wanted to hear more of it.

This isn't the man Savannah wanted you to be.

Guy lurched away from Amy's corpse. His heart thundered like a war drum. The satisfaction had vanished; in its place was horror and nausea.

He blinked as his vision resolved. He was breathless. Hot, sticky blood drenched his arms and face. Amy was no longer recognizable as human. He'd severed her arm, gouged a hole in her face, and smashed every rib. Blood mingled with the red dress and pooled across the tile floor. Guy unfurled his fingers. They shook as a bone fragment dripped off his thumb. A muffled sob slipped out of him.

I don't want to be a violent man. I don't want to be like her.

The two faceless children stood in the doorway. Guy hadn't seen them enter. He knew they weren't real, but he still recoiled, ashamed of what they'd witnessed.

The children quivered then crumbled, like two perfect sand-castles that had dried out. Their forms disintegrated into the floor, until there was nothing of them left.

The room shook. Guy staggered to his feet as paint fell off the walls in thick flakes. The fridge aged and discolored. The tiles chipped. The window darkened with grime. Guy grabbed at the counter as his suit rippled into the rain-soaked work clothes. Red blooms soaked the fabric, and with them came the burning pain of the stab wounds Amy had inflicted before dragging him into her fantasy world. Rookward shook a final time then settled, returned to its true form.

Amy stood behind him. Her face was a pulp. One arm hung low, nearly severed except for a thin strip of flesh. White ribs poked out of the hole in her chest.

Guy moaned in growing horror and grabbed one of the knives out of its chopping block. Age had stuck it to the wood, and he had to shake it to get it free. The fight had drained his energy, and blood continued to seep from the wounds in his chest and back. He wasn't yet willing to give in to the insane woman, though.

The illusion faded from Amy at last. Color left her skin. The shredded red dress and jewelry crumbled. They drifted away from her like soot caught in the wind, revealing the gray slip dress. Underneath the illusion, her body was intact. All signs of the violence melted away. The white cataracts grew across her eyes, and the silky black hair became matted and oily.

Understanding hit Guy, but it wasn't a happy revelation. *When she pulls me into her fantasy, she creates an alternate reality. Nothing from the real world has any influence on it...and whatever I do inside the fantasy has no impact on the real world.*

Amy bellowed, fury ringing through the air and hurting Guy's ears. He flinched. The kitchen was changing, its walls bowing in like a paper box being crumpled. He started for the door, but it slammed shut. Vines grew through the thin gap below the wood. They writhed as they extended their tendrils toward Guy. He tried to move back from them, but the tiles slid out from under his feet, and he collapsed to the ground.

Amy loomed over him, her lips bent into a snarl. When she opened her mouth, the inside was black, and the teeth were sharpened into points. A thick, obsidian liquid oozed from around the jaws.

"You *coward.*" She sounded barely human.

Guy slashed the knife toward her but missed. She grabbed the neck of his shirt and tossed him through the doorway and into the dining room as though he weighed nothing.

Guy hit one of the chairs and crumpled to the ground. The knife skittered out of his hand, and pain flared through already-aching muscles. He struggled to draw air. Amy followed him, the black liquid leaking from her nose and dribbling over twisted lips.

"Why do you do this?" She dropped herself on top of him, pressing him into the floor with her knees. Her bony hands wrapped around his throat. "Traitorous, cruel creature. You *love* me."

He strained to speak, but the pressure on his throat choked off his voice. He beat at her cold, bloodless arms, but she didn't seem to notice. The glint of metal pulled his attention to the knife, which lay on the floor just above his head.

"We are destined to be together," Amy hissed. She leaned closer, her blackened lips just inches from his. "Why must you torment me so?"

His scrabbling fingers touched the knife. His lungs ached, but he threw all of his remaining strength into sweeping his arm up. The knife plunged through Amy's neck, angled up to pierce her skull.

Her snarl vanished. The tightness around Guy's throat loosened, and he managed to suck in oxygen. Amy's gaunt cheeks fluttered as she tried to speak through the knife embedded in her throat.

"I never loved you," Guy spat. "You heartless, soulless monster."

She opened her jaw—whether to speak or scream, Guy never knew. Her form bubbled as though a million insects were trapped under the skin, writhing and desperate to be free. The gray tint of her flesh darkened, taking on a green hue as she tilted her head back, eyes bulging and jaw stretched wide in horror.

Then the cut in her throat widened, splitting down her torso and across her skull. The flesh frayed at the edges, desiccating, becoming dust—the same dust that permeated every one of the house's pores—and tumbled away. Spiders spilled out of the sack. They rolled over Guy, billions of legs twitching, like a blanket out of a waking nightmare. It was all he could do to squeeze his eyes closed and seal his lips. But they scattered quickly, unwilling to linger on him. He cracked his eyes open in time to see the last of Amy's shell blow away as dust, dissipating through the rooms, the final remains of the woman who had owned Rookward for fifty years.

She was half-alive. I am half-dead. I suppose that was enough.

Guy managed a final, twitching smile as he lay back among the scattering spiders and a growing pool of his own blood.

CHAPTER 32

A HIGH-PITCHED NOISE FILLED Guy's ears. He opened his eyes a fraction and blinked at the seemingly endless white surrounding him.

So this is death.

He wasn't as frightened as he'd expected to be.

Do I have regrets? That was an easy question to answer. Of course; he didn't believe a single human could pass over without at least a handful. But the ones that rose to the forefront of his mind were especially bitter.

He hated what this would do to his mother. He wished he'd told her he loved her more often. He wished he could have made her proud.

Then he thought of Savannah. He should have tried harder for her. Not just before the accident, but after. Instead of hiding from the shame and guilt, he should have found a way to redeem himself. She was one of the best things to ever happen to him, and he'd let her slip away.

And his baby daughter…he still didn't know her name. He would never have the chance to go to her recitals, to braid her hair, to play dress-up, or draw her height onto the kitchen doorframe.

He hoped that if a broken man like him could be allowed into heaven, they would give him a way to watch over his family. If he couldn't be with them, he wanted to at least cherish their lives and cheer for their triumphs.

A face swam into view above him, disturbing the perfect white. To Guy's shock, it didn't have a mouth. The eyes crinkled as they met his, though, then a booming voice was saying, "Hey, we've got a fighter."

What's there left to fight? Amy's gone. Thomas and his family can have peace. I'm done; now I just want to rest.

A second voice spoke. "Hang on a bit longer, buddy. We're almost there."

He finally recognized the blaring noise. Sirens. The white surrounding him was the ambulance's walls and ceiling. And the face wasn't missing its mouth—it was wearing a mask.

Guy chuckled, even though it hurt. *They answered my call after all. Fancy that.*

The days following were a blur. Two rounds of surgery, multiple blood transfusions, and a course of strong antibiotics stabilized

Guy. As soon as he was strong enough to talk for an extended period, the police arrived to question him about Tiff. He told them as much of the truth as he thought they would believe: she'd visited with her boyfriend then came back alone two nights later. Guy hadn't heard her second arrival or seen the tree fall on her; he'd only discovered them in the morning, at which time, he crashed his pickup truck in his grief and urgency to leave.

Guy suspected they didn't fully believe him. His fingerprints were all over the insides of Tiff's car, bag, and phone, and according to the senior officer, her car keys had been found discarded in the grass twenty paces from her body. Plus, Guy knew his history with Savannah didn't paint him in a positive light. But there was no evidence to suggest Tiff's death hadn't been natural, as improbable as the event was.

Then came a harder question: Who had stabbed him? Again, Guy plumbed for something near honesty, simply because it was easier to keep his story straight. He told them a strange woman had stabbed him. He didn't know who she was or why she was at Rookward, but he intimated she might have been on drugs. When asked what she looked like, he described Amy's appearance on the final night, when she'd worn the red dress and waltzed through the house with him. Again, he could see skepticism on the police officers' faces. It didn't help that there was no DNA evidence or fingerprints in the building besides Guy's.

He was referred for a mental health evaluation and told not to leave the area for a few weeks while they checked his story. Then, mercifully, they left him in peace.

Heather sat by Guy's bed every day while he was in the hospital. She arrived as soon as visiting hours began and only left when they ended, and always brought a bagful of books and freshly baked food for him. Guy could see the stress had worn on her. He repeatedly told her to stay home, but no amount of begging could stop her from making the trip to visit him every day. Just like after Savannah's accident, she accepted his account of what happened at Rookward without even a hint of doubt. It made Guy's heart ache with gratitude.

The stay in the hospital gave Guy a lot of time to think. He considered Rookward's future. Even though he believed Amy had been excised from the house, he didn't want to step foot in the building ever again. He'd made some improvements during his six days at Rookward House but also caused a lot of new problems, not least of all the blood he'd dripped everywhere. The building wouldn't be valued as highly as he'd initially hoped, but it wouldn't be worthless, either. They would sell it as-is, take the hit on the profit, and move to whatever place they could afford. Depending on what the real estate agent could wrangle, Guy and his mother might need to rent for a few months until he could get a stable income and save up enough for a good deposit. The thought wasn't as bitter as it might have once been. They were still together, and Guy knew they would make it work—somehow.

Then, not long after the doctors started talking about Guy being close to going home, his mother arrived with some news that turned his plans upside down.

She peeked into the room and gave him a nervous, hesitant smile. He put his book aside and sat up a little straighter in the bed. "What is it?"

"It's, uh…" She glanced behind herself and nudged her glasses up her nose. "It's Savannah."

He felt as though someone had smacked his heart with a baseball bat. "What? Is she okay?"

Heather moved closer, hands clenched and an apologetic smile pulling at her mouth. "Oh yes, of course she is. It's just, when the paramedics found you, they also found the notes you'd left on the table. You were in the ICU at the time, and we didn't know if you would pull through, so I mailed your note to Savannah. I'm sorry, I know I should have waited to see if it was what you wanted—but I thought I was doing the right thing at the time. And, well, she's come to visit."

"Oh." He'd completely forgotten about the messages. Heat rushed across his face, and he became acutely aware that he hadn't brushed his hair that morning, and that stubble had started to grow.

Motion drew his eyes to the doorway. Savannah stood there, golden hair caught in the light as she brushed it behind her ear. Her cheeks were pale, but otherwise, she looked healthy. Better than healthy—she was stunning. Guy didn't know if she'd done it intentionally, but she'd worn his favorite dress, the red summer frock with the sweetheart neckline. And she cradled a tiny, pink-clad baby in her arms.

Guy didn't know what to say. His throat ached, and his eyes

burned. He forced his tongue to move, but all that came out was a lame "I'm so sorry."

Savannah's eyebrows pulled together, and her lips tightened. Some kind of emotion was growing inside her, and Guy's heart skipped a beat. He clenched his fists into the bed sheets, preparing for disdain or even anger.

But then she said, "I miss you," and Guy's burning eyes overflowed.

ABOUT THE AUTHOR

Darcy Coates is the *USA Today* bestselling author of *Hunted*, *The Haunting of Ashburn House*, *Craven Manor*, and more than a dozen horror and suspense titles. She lives on the Central Coast of Australia with her family, cats, and a garden full of herbs and vegetables. Darcy loves forests, especially old-growth forests where the trees dwarf anyone who steps between them. Wherever she lives, she tries to have a mountain range close by.

THE HAUNTING OF
BLACKWOOD HOUSE

HOW LONG COULD YOU SURVIVE?

As the daughter of spiritualists, Mara's childhood was filled with séances and scam mediums. Now she's ready to start over with her fiancé, Neil, far away from the superstitions she's learned to loathe...but her past isn't willing to let her go so easily. And neither is Blackwood House.

When Mara and Neil purchased the derelict property, they were warned that ever since the murder of its original owner, things have changed. Strange shadows stalk the halls. Doors creak open by themselves. Voices whisper in the night. And watchful eyes follow her every move. But Mara's convinced she can't possibly be in danger. Because ghosts aren't real...are they?

THE HOUSE NEXT DOOR

NO ONE STAYS HERE FOR LONG.

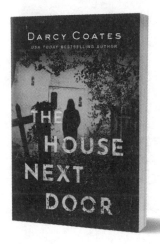

Josephine began to suspect something was wrong with the house next door when its family fled in the middle of the night, the children screaming, the mother crying. They never came back. No family stays at Marwick House for long. No life lingers beyond its blackened windows. No voices drift from its ancient halls. Once, Josephine swore she saw a woman's silhouette pacing through the upstairs room...but that's impossible. No one had been there in a long, long time.

But now someone new has moved next door, and Marwick House is slowly waking up. Torn between staying away and warning the new tenant, Josephine only knows that if she isn't careful, she may be its next victim...

CRAVEN MANOR

SOME SECRETS ARE BETTER LEFT FORGOTTEN.

Daniel is desperate for a fresh start. So when a mysterious figure offers the position of groundskeeper at an ancient estate, he leaps at the chance. Alarm bells start ringing when he arrives at Craven Manor. The abandoned mansion's front door hangs open, and leaves and cobwebs coat the marble foyer. It's clear no one has lived here in a long time... but he has nowhere else to go.

Against his better judgment, he moves into the groundskeeper's cottage tucked away behind the old family crypt. But when a candle flickers to life in the abandoned tower window, Daniel realizes he isn't alone after all. Craven Manor is hiding a terrible secret... One that threatens to bury him with it.